G000117588

For my mother
Who bought me a beautiful journal about two years ago and told me with a knowing look when I asked what it was for, "Your book. It's time for you to start." I love you, Momma. Thanks for always believing in me, even when I didn't believe in myself.

For my Pawpaw
You may not be here today, but I think you always knew I would write. Thank you for showing me that reading was the coolest and most admirable hobby. You are forever in my heart.

For my sister, father, and loving husband who spent hours reading and editing this book to help make my dream come true. You are the real rockstars.

Dreamwalkers

Dreamwalkers

Brooke Terry

© Copyright 2021 Brooke Terry
All rights reserved.

No portion of this book may be reproduced in whole or
in part, by any means whatsoever, except for passages
excerpted for the purposes of review, without the prior
written permission of the publisher.

For information, or to order additional copies, please
contact:

Beacon Publishing Group
P.O. Box 41573 Charleston, S.C. 29423
800.817.8480| beaconpublishinggroup.com

Publisher's catalog available by request.

ISBN-13: 978-1-949472-34-9

ISBN-10: 1-949472-34-9

Published in 2021. New York, NY 10001.

First Edition. Printed in the USA.

The Realm of ♦

Arvenia

Illustrated by Meagan Bragwell

Only with darkness, may we truly understand the light.

TABLE OF CONTENTS

PROLOGUE
500 Years Ago

The sun beat down on the city of Avendale as its citizens went about their daily duties and activities. The bustle of the morning was nearing a close as the morning dew started to evaporate in the heat. Aryn found himself jostled at every turn as he tried to navigate the crowd of people in the market. Finally reaching the stall he wanted, Aryn stopped to look at the fresh fruits available. He pointed to a stack of large yellow and red apples and traded two bronze coins for them. As Aryn placed two of his three apples in the bag hanging over his shoulder, he shook his head. He could have been just now waking up in his feather bed to the smells of a hearty breakfast instead of eating apples.

Aryn sighed and turned in the direction of his family's townhome that was about four blocks from the market. He didn't mind helping his father occasionally, but lately, his father had demanded his help every day, usually before the first rays of sunlight broke through the morning mists. Aryn had been traveling as far as the Dunbar River to deliver the multitude of letters his father imparted to him. Each morning, his father would wake Aryn by placing another large stack at the end of his bed. This was the eighth day Aryn had been conscripted into delivering the letters.

Aryn did not think of himself as particularly curious, but he had noticed the odd looks on the faces of the recipients of the letters. As the days went by and the stacks kept coming, Aryn could not shake the feeling that maybe the pages held some information that was unwelcome.

Aryn took another large bite from the apple as he neared his front door. He could hear his mother yelling for his little sister, Salia, to help ready the midday meal. It was later in the day than Aryn had thought. He stifled a yawn as he opened the door. His thoughts drifted from the letters to his bed that beckoned him from the second floor.

***

A rough shake had Aryn sitting bolt-upright in his bed. His blanket fell off his shoulders as he gasped. The room was almost pitch black around him, except for a small candle lighting an unfriendly face. His father, dressed in his captain's uniform, stood over him. Despite being his blood relation, Aryn felt the intimidation at this moment that he supposed all of Captain Darius's men felt while on duty.

"Aryn, get up. We need to leave as soon as you are dressed." Darius said, his voice rough with sleep. His father was a burly man and stood around six feet tall. He had wide shoulders and a trim waist, which was unusual in men his age. Aryn was always proud of his father when the man put on his uniform, but by gods, why did he have it on in the middle of the night?

Darius had been promoted to captain of the city guard almost seven years before. It had changed Aryn's family's way of life. Aryn was thankful for his father's promotion because it had meant better tutors for his siblings. It also promised no more restless nights after a meager dinner split between five people. But, never in the last seven years had he woken him in the middle of the night for guard duties. Aryn was only fifteen and not technically a part of the ranks. He was only brought in as a regular messenger.

Aryn sat confused and stared as his father turned to walk out of his door. The captain looked back and raised a hand, motioning him to hurry. *Always giving orders.* Aryn shook his head in confusion and rose. He stared longingly at his bed as he pulled on a clean pair of trousers and buttoned up his shirt. At this rate, he was not likely to ever get a full nights' sleep. Aryn followed his father downstairs into the kitchen. Darius lifted a sheet of mail from the table and draped it silently over Aryn's shoulders. This was starting to get serious. "Why do I need this?" Aryn whispered. Queasiness rolled through his stomach.

"Our errand tonight involves danger, so I would like you to be protected." His father turned to grab a few more items from the table. When he turned around once more, Aryn started. Darius held a pair of heavy boots, a sword, and a helm. "You need to look the part, and we need as many hands as we can find, boy." His father thrust the items into Aryn's arms before walking out of the kitchen.

"But, where are we going?" Aryn asked as he gripped tightly to his new bundle of equipment. It was too late. The captain had already walked through the door to begin saddling their horses.

***

Aryn glanced around as he held onto his saddle with sweaty palms. His father was riding at the front of a very long line of soldiers. A few citizens, dressed in dark clothing and carrying no weapons, were behind the soldiers. Aryn hadn't bothered asking any more questions. Darius had simply glared at him when he had repeated his last one. He knew by now that he would not get any answers.

***

The sun had been up for about two hours. Aryn could feel the lack of sleep muddling his mind. As they reached the top of the hill up ahead, he was surprised to see small cabins. The cabins stretched on for miles and miles. *Terra?* He thought to himself. He had never been this far east, but he had heard of the King's decision to make these lands part of Arvenia. The procession halted, drawing Aryn's attention back to those ahead of him. One of the citizens in black urged his steed into a trot to the front of the guard. Once he reached the summit of the hill, he dismounted and dug into his saddle bag.

Aryn couldn't make out the retrieved item, though he could see the man cut his hand and let blood fall onto the ground. The figure fell to his knees, raised his hands into the air, and began chanting in an odd language. Aryn glanced around nervously at the others beside him. They looked just as terrified as he felt. Magic was forbidden in Arvenia.

The man continued his chanting. Aryn noticed that the sun, which had been so bright only moments before, was retreating behind a massive black object in the sky. *Could it be an eclipse?* As darkness fell over the cabins up ahead, the horses began to panic. Whispered voices could be heard throughout the line of soldiers as they calmed their anxious steeds. Aryn glanced around as his unease grew. *Who was that man?*

The strange man rose to his feet and turned to face the line of soldiers and citizens behind him. He let out a booming voice.

"It has begun!"

Aryn saw his father begin distributing strange amulets or…crystals? The men took one and passed the remaining crystals to the soldiers behind themselves in the line. When they were handed to him, Aryn passed the whole bundle on. Several minutes passed before the strange man spoke again.

"You know what you must do. You know what you must protect your people from! Let us retrieve them, so we ensure that our enemies don't overtake us in the dark!"

With this exclamation, the men kicked their steeds and directed them towards the cabins up ahead. Aryn watched in shock as doors were ripped from their hinges and people were dragged out of their homes. He turned to see if anyone else was watching. Darius urged his steed back towards Aryn's.

"Come, Aryn. We have work to do."

He shook his head as his father held out an extra crystal for him to take. Aryn looked at him in shock, which was returned with a blank stare. They were interrupted by a man riding up to address the captain. "Captain, the crystals are working like the King said they would, but some have escaped. What should we do about them?"

"Find them. You have the orders. None left alive." At this statement, Aryn's eyes widened in horror. His father turned back to him.

"You have no idea what we have uncovered here, Aryn. This is in the best interest for Arvenia's people." Aryn listened to his father's words as he watched a young boy, around his own age, get carried from his cabin by three guards. The guards laid him on the ground and touched his forehead with a crystal. Aryn could see the crystal glow in the darkness. The guards continued to hold the boy down until he stopped fighting. Aryn knew he would never be rid of the horror of the boy's screams echoing throughout the hills.

ONE
Present Day
Ansley

In the darkness, Ansley leaned back against the wooden shed and tried to slow her breathing. Just when she needed silence, her heart seemed to beat out a rhythm loud enough for the deaf to hear. She focused on taking measured breaths and blowing them back out slowly, but her heart continued its traitorous mission to reveal her location.

She crept out from the cover of the utility shed she had scrambled towards only moments ago and glanced around the corner. Ansley could barely see anything in the darkness, but she knew who was out there. She quickly retreated behind her temporary haven to refocus on her breathing. Horror filled her as the sleeve of her cotton shirt caught on the jagged boards of the shed. She took a deep breath as her fingers worked to free her arm.

Where had he gone? He was there somewhere. She hoped that he wasn't coming around the other side of the building to surprise her. Anticipating that fate and the dangers of being caught, Ansley began to move slowly along the building in the other direction. Her breath caught in her throat, and her heart began tap-dancing as she heard footsteps running in the direction of the shed. Her heart stopped suddenly, and a gasp escaped from her lips.

"Come out, you stupid little girl!" The man snarled as he prowled around the edge of the shed nearest to her.

Ansley was not certain where she was or how she had gotten here. Worse, she wasn't sure that there were any buildings or woods nearby to run towards. When she had approached the shed, it had been the only structured in sight for miles around her in the dark. She shouldn't have volunteered for this. Ansley's family had been tracking this group of shifters for weeks. She'd foolishly thought that she could help apprehend them. Her hands shook in the darkness, and she could see her breath as it escaped her lips. Ansley silently wished that she had her bow. She knew that she could easily take down her assailant if she had the weapon in her hands.

She was afraid, but she knew she could not linger here forever. Taking a deep breath, Ansley ran out from behind the shed to take her chances and stopped upon seeing her pursuer. She tried to draw herself up taller to give the impression of strength, but it was useless. The man in front of her easily stood at six feet tall. She barely reached five. She was no match for him in any way.

He gave her a knowing grin as she stared at him helplessly. His shoulders were broad, and his arms rippled with unleashed potential. This was a stark contrast to Ansley, who at 18 years old, was small and slender. Her arms were thin but strong enough to do the farm work often required of them. He held a large sword out towards her, and he sneered at her the same way a fox may look at his dinner. In a few seconds, the sword was swallowed by a flame that reached from hilt to tip. Ansley reached nervously inside her coat to give the impression that she was holding a weapon.

The man let out a deep throaty laugh. "Give it up, girl. We both know you are unarmed and alone out here. Let's get this over with already. I want to enjoy the rest of my night." His malicious grin was broken up by his tongue running over his teeth.

Repulsed, Ansley backed away from him, and her heartbeat thrummed throughout her body as a cold sweat dripped down the back of her neck. Her arms erupted in goosebumps. A chill ran through her blood. She never thought her life would end this way. She had barely even begun to experience anything, and now it was being ripped away so easily. She swallowed what she could of her fear and prepared herself for the worst.

In a single moment, lightning from an approaching storm lit up the sky, and the downpour began to cover her in a coat of sweet summer rain. The cold that had wrapped around her was lost, blown away like a feather in the wind. She felt hope fill her soul and believed she was no longer alone. Ansley lifted *her face to the sky and let the soft rain roll down her face to calm her nerves. A familiar shadow approached from behind the man, hands outstretched out in his direction. Ansley dared to hope that another ending was in store for her.*

As the rain fell on the man's grimy, shoulder-length hair, he seemed to sense the change in Ansley's attitude and the atmosphere itself. He half-turned, but it wasn't quick enough to stop what was coming. A small, round pit opened up in the earth under his feet, sending him soaring to the bottom with a clash. Heavy tree roots sprang from the soil and barred the pit's opening. Ansley could hear the man's growls below. She thought the noises sounded like those of a caged lion, but she supposed he was close enough to an animal to react like one. She frowned, not losing sight of how lucky she had been.

Then, she turned to find a soft, wrinkled hand on her shoulder, and a smile on the face of the person reaching out to her. Her grandmother whispered over the rain, "Come, child."

***

Ansley gasped for breath as her eyes sprang open. She sat up in her small, quilt-covered bed and shook her head at the terror flooding her body. It still amazed her how everything could feel so real inside of the dreams, only to return to her reality.

Dreamwalkers

Her father liked to call it "out of body", but that did not make it any less shocking when she returned from walking each morning. She thought about the transition and wondered if anyone had successfully proven if the soul of a dreamwalker actually left their body at night. If so, it would leave the body very vulnerable, but she knew that was the case anyway. Her father had taught her that every time the dream realm was entered, that became the reality. The body would always suffer the consequences of what happened to the soul. At least, that is what she had always been told. She had been lucky thus far to not have to learn the truth of the matter. She stretched her arms over her head to accompany a wide yawn before tidying her shoulder length black hair, which had knotted itself in the night.

Ansley swung her legs over the side of her bed and felt comforted when her feet touched the cool wooden floorboards. It brought her back to reality. She inhaled the familiar scents of her childhood: lavender and coffee.

Lavender was her mother's favorite plant to grow, and it had sprung up at her hands all around the family's farm. Each morning, Ansley's father also insisted that they welcome each other back from their dream adventures with a steaming hot cup of coffee. She loved that about him. Smiling in anticipation of her awaiting cup, she stood and grabbed her shawl.

Always needing to be rescued! She was tired of that, but she wasn't sure it would change any over the coming months with her inheritance ceremony looming.

Ansley plodded down the hallway trying to shake off the memory of the night spent running from her assailant. She was thankful that her parents had not been involved. She smiled again as she was pulled from her musings by the sound of her younger brothers running into the kitchen ahead.

Their kitchen was fairly large for the size of their home. It had a large black stove and lots of countertops for Ansley's mother to prepare the meals they all savored. Ansley glanced at the kitchen with new eyes, as if returning for the first time after a long journey. One large, rectangular kitchen table took up the majority of the space. But, there was still enough room on each side for her brothers to play their usual morning game of "Chase" around the table.

Ansley rolled her eyes at them as she watched Eli, her youngest brother, running ahead of Ryker while holding a piece of jelly-smeared toast as high above his head as his arm could reach. Ryker kept reaching for it, but Eli was too fast. Despite turning nine in the next few weeks, Ryker was still prey to his younger brother's games. Eli's bright blue eyes twinkled with wicked delight as he weaved and bobbed around his father and mother to avoid Ryker's angry hands.

"Mom!!" Ryker yelled in frustration. Leila briefly turned her head away from the coffee pot that was poised over her empty cup to glance in his direction. She was a slight woman, but she was tall. Ansley had always thought she favored her mother most. Her mother's long, black, wavy hair, and slender frame had been passed on to her; however, Ansley's bright, lagoon blue eyes had been inherited from her father. She shared the same eyes as Eli, who had climbed on the table and was now laughing hysterically while pointing at Ryker. Leila had always said that her and Ryker's brown eyes came from her father, whom Ansley never had the chance to meet before he passed on.

"E-if I have to come over there, you will regret it," Leila simply said, eyeing her unruly toddler. He stopped mid-laugh and looked at her nervously. She might've been soft-spoken, but the woman could command an army with the look she gave that little monster. Eli finally gave in and handed his brother the toast while climbing down off the table.

"Finally! You grace us with your presence!" Ansley's father, Everett, boomed across the room. Ansley turned in his direction and smiled sweetly. She then headed for the row of clean coffee cups. "Please, do tell us of your adventures from last night?" He inquired as he sipped his steaming cup. His eyes sparkled mischievously, as if he already knew exactly what had happened.

"It wasn't anything special…" Ansley murmured into her coffee cup. She added two creams and one sugar to the black brew.

Everett was a burly man, but he could undo an opponent with more than just his strength. He could outwit anyone Ansley had met. Ansley watched the cogs turning behind his wrinkled, tan brow as he looked over her, determining if she had sustained any injuries from her dream.

Ansley's father had always had a way with her. Being the only girl in the house besides her mother, Ansley might've been inclined to have little in common with her father. In reality, Ansley and her father shared much more than either of her siblings: a sharp mind, a sense of humor, and unbending stubbornness.

"Oh really?" Everett exclaimed. "Then, why do I get the feeling I will be hearing more from Nana at dinner tonight?"

"Think what you want, Daddy," Ansley said with a smile. "I have chores to do at Nana's."

"Be careful and ask Nana if she is still planning to make the pie for dinner tonight. I have her blueberries picked and ready." Leila said over her shoulder as she continued to wash the breakfast dishes.

"I'll be back in a few hours." Ansley said in her father's direction.

"Take your time. Nana gets lonely these days." Everett replied as he kissed his daughter on the forehead and walked back towards his bedroom to change into his work clothes.

Ansley walked down the hall to her own bedroom. She was happy for an opportunity to avoid discussing her dream with her parents, but that didn't change the fact that her grandmother would be eagerly awaiting her when she arrived. She sighed as she changed into a pair of supple work pants and a worn, button-up shirt. She knew that her grandmother would want to go over each error that led to Ansley being cornered by the shifter.

She grabbed her shoulder bag from the chair near her bed and headed back out towards the kitchen. Ansley snagged a few apples for an afternoon snack and placed them in her bag. She didn't wait to say goodbye to her family, choosing to sneak out the door in hopes of avoiding more confrontation.

Ansley took a deep breath of the fresh morning air and looked out at the land her family had lived on for generations. To the north, she could see the Dream Hollow Mountains rising from the clouds, and as far as she could see to the east were cottages, much like her own. The sunlight kissed each mountain peak like a mother waking up her sleeping child to begin the day.

The land had been settled for hundreds of years after Avendale had gone through one of the worst famines known in history. Terra, originally called Raynan for its peaceful nature, was a small valley at the foot of the Dream Hollow Mountains that fell just outside the capital city of Avendale. Raynan had been inhabited for centuries by native people who lived off the land. These people relied mostly on hunting and gathering for sustenance but had no idea of the wealth of soil that lay below the sprawling grasslands.

After the famine had hit Avendale and resulted in the deaths of almost half of the population, the King declared the land would be turned into farmlands. He wrote a formal decree, gifting the lands to the natives living on it with only one request: that they farm and share their crops with the surrounding cities. Thus, Terra was created and renamed to honor its new purpose, and the tribes became actual citizens of the kingdom.

None of these thoughts filled Ansley's head as she inhaled the familiar smells surrounding her. She let the wafts of grasses, flowers, and morning dew steady her as she formally greeted the morning.

Life in these mountains was never about splendor. It was about tradition, duty, and family. Her family had decided to settle near her grandmother because the rainfall was ideal for growing her father's specialty: corn. Little did he know that the land would also support her mother's lilies of the valley.

Ansley began walking west over the rolling hills to her grandmother's house. She trailed her hands through the tall grasses and softly swaying wildflowers.

Each touch was welcoming and pulled her deeper into the world that had felt so distant last night. She heaved another sigh thinking once more of her near-defeat. *Let's get this lecture started already,* she thought to herself.

Ansley knocked on the door and entered the small kitchen to find her grandmother leaning over the stove and stirring a large pot of oats. Ansley's grandmother, Bianca, was nearing her seventieth year, but like most dreamwalkers, her age was only a number. She was tall like her son Everett, and she was strong. Her arms endured hours of farm work now that she lived alone. Her grey hair was wavy and long but kept neat in a bun at the base of her neck. As usual, Bianca was dressed in black leather work boots, riding pants, and a work shirt. Her grandmother was contrary to every image Ansley could attribute to being an *actual* grandmother, but it suited her.

Ansley did not like oatmeal, but her grandmother insisted that it was the best way to feed the mind after a long and trying night. Bianca turned and looked at her with a smile flooding her face. "Good morning, Starlight. How are you feeling?"

Ansley scowled but did not answer. She walked to the table and sat down at the cup of coffee already waiting for her. Her second cup for the morning. Her cream already sat in a small pitcher beside the steaming cup.

"Well, I thought I would start breakfast early this morning. I knew you would need a pick-me-up after our adventure." Her grandmother tried again.

"*My* adventure you mean. *You* didn't volunteer for a mission you weren't prepared for. *You* didn't chase after one of the rebel shifters by yourself, and *you* didn't almost lead us into a situation where you were easily cornered without a skill to protect yourself." Ansley's unhappiness hung over the room like a dark thundercloud as her grandmother digested this statement.

"We all make mistakes starting out, dear. It is of no consequence that you did. You must learn and try to be more wary in the future. It's common for a walker's naivety to betray them before an inheritance ceremony. Besides, nothing that you did will hinder our attempts to find those rebels. They will be brought to justice as our elders have deemed necessary for the crimes they have committed." Bianca picked up her own coffee cup and took a small sip, "Believe it or not, I do remember my own experiences before my ceremony. Even *I* made a few mistakes." She winked at Ansley as she turned back to the pot, spooning out two bowls of breakfast. She added chopped nuts, blueberries, honey, and a strawberry to the top of the bowls before bringing them to the table.

She placed a bowl in front of Ansley and sat down on the opposite side of the table. Ansley's skin raised in goosebumps as a memory flashed before her eyes...

***

Leila was sitting in Ansley's place as a little girl ran into the kitchen. Her grandmother and mother were eating oatmeal, much like Ansley and Bianca were this morning. Everett walked into the kitchen, finished with his morning chores.

"Good morning, Starlight!!" His voice rumbled as the little Ansley ran into his arms. He lifted her high into the air, and his laughter boomed out over her giggles.

"Don't send her head through the ceiling," Leila said into her bowl of oatmeal with a small smile, "We don't want to have to search the skies for her." Everett laughed again and put Ansley on her two small feet. She ran quickly toward her grandmother, who hoisted her up on her lap and promptly gave her a bite of hot, sweet oatmeal.

***

Ansley felt an odd feeling in her gut as she took a sip of coffee. Her uneasiness did not disappear with her memory.

"Ansley?" Nana asked as her face became clear again, noticing her grandaughter's distraction. Bianca's eyes were filled with concern. "Are you nervous about the ceremony?" She inquired softly, reaching over her coffee cup and placing her hand on Ansley's.

20

"No, Nana. I know it will be alright. You'll be there with me anyway, so what could go wrong?" Ansley said as she took a bite of honey and strawberries, trying to push aside her unease.

The ceremony was rapidly approaching, and it was really all she had thought about for years. Ansley had turned eighteen earlier in the fall. Her family finally agreed it was time. The ceremony, more formally called "the inheritance ceremony," was only performed for dreamwalkers over the age of eighteen. This was to ensure that the young ones were ready for the responsibility attributed to the skills.

Prior to the ceremony, a dreamwalker could only appear in dreams of family members or those who had invited them. Children usually began showing signs around the age of ten to twelve and were invited to their parents' dreams to begin training.

Then there were the others. *The elite*, they were called. They were born with skills and did not have to participate in an inheritance ceremony. Their skills were acquired directly from the gods, and they were said to be the strongest of all dreamwalkers.

Ansley took another bite as she mused over the term. As a child, she had eagerly waited to see if she was an elite, but she had never shown signs of skills. Her training had begun when she was only nine. The years were littered with memories of nights much like the last and mornings spent discussing the rights and wrongs of each walk. Ansley's thoughts turned to her parents as she hastily scooped the last few bites of oats from her bowl. She washed it down with the warm coffee and took her dishes to the sink.

"I know you worry for me, but I would rather not think about this at the moment. The ceremony will come and pass, and I would rather not stress over the details just yet." She walked back to her grandmother and hugged her tightly around the neck. When Ansley pulled away from her, a grey hair tickled her cheek.

Bianca planted a kiss on Ansley's forehead. "Go home, Ansley, and tend to your duties with your father. I will handle my chores for the morning, and we will talk more later. I love you, Starlight," she said softly. She released her granddaughter, who did as she was told and walked to the door. Ansley turned one last time.

"I never can understand why you, Dad, and Mother are always so worried about the ceremony. You have been preparing me for years, and I am only the first! Ryker and Eli will have to follow someday too," she said as she opened the door to leave.

Bianca smiled. "Yes, but you are the first of theirs to inherit. Surely, you can understand a parent's worry?" A tear glistened on her cheek.

Ansley softened her tone, "Yes, but you've spent years training me, so I know that whatever the future holds, I'll be ready." She shared one last smile with her grandmother before stepping outside.

Ansley strolled slowly back through the fields, oblivious to most of her surroundings. She was lost in thought over what her grandmother had been saying. She spotted her family's cottage and small farm ahead and smiled despite herself. She could already imagine Eli running around her father as he tried to finish his morning chores.

Eli was merely three years old, but he already had such a strong will. Ryker, though, was a soft-natured boy. He never yelled or cried much as a young child. As he grew older, his interest in animals had grown. His soft-spoken manner could calm even the unruliest horse. Ansley was eager to see if his skills would start to emerge after his upcoming birthday. Not all in a dreamwalker's family were blessed with emerging, but it was more of a rarity when they did not. Emergence meant that there was potential for skill, and those children could tolerate an inheritance from a family member one day. Ansley yearned to no longer be the only one training in her home.

But Ryker might've been elite. Ansley struggled to remember what her father had said about it, *"It is very rare, but possible."* He had gone on to explain that no one had been born elite in over one hundred years in their family. Finally, Ansley had understood his meaning of rare.

Ansley eased down the sloping hills, and she listened for the happy sounds that she always associated with her home. It was oddly quiet. She was puzzled by this but did not dwell on the thought. Their family had never been a subdued one. With the miles between them and their neighbors, it did not matter much. The softly rolling hills absorbed any sounds, keeping their secrets from listening ears.

As Ansley drew closer, she was startled to notice that the door was open. Her mother had but one rule in the house that was strictly enforced. *Keep the door closed.* Their skills made her mother cautious, and she always worried that someone would overhear them talking about something walking related.

Ansley felt her heart stop as she stood and stared at the open door. Finally, she began running. When she glanced inside, she cried out in horror. Her hand shook and lingered over her mouth as tears welled in her eyes. She looked into the kitchen, and her vision began to grow blurry.

Blood pooled on the floor in a circle under the large wooden table. Sweet Eli lay under it face up with his brilliant blue eyes looking forever at the stars. Ryker lay next to him on his side, almost frozen in time with his arm outstretched for a short blade that laid on the floor. His blood-coated fingers were touching his father's arm. Everett, like Eli, laid face up with those same blue eyes staring up at whoever had attacked his family. The sight of her father was even more shocking to Ansley. His face had been lively and young only hours before. Wrinkles now marred his once-smooth face, and his hair had turned a light grey. It looked as if he had aged over thirty years in the hours since she had seen him last.

Ansley looked down upon her father and noticed suddenly that no marks were on him. He was untouched but obviously dead. *How odd…*she found herself thinking as if simply viewing the scene through another's eyes. Spots flickered across her vision as she turned away from her brothers and father. As she walked around the table, she spotted her mother. Anguish tugged heavily on her heart. Ansley let out a loud sob and sunk to the ground.

Leila lay face down with her beautiful, waist-long hair strewn out over her. Hers had also turned. In contrast to Everett's hair, Leila's was now a dark, foreboding gray. Her wrinkled and aged hands were reaching in the direction of her dear husband, whose hand she would no longer hold. Ansley saw no marks on her either, but she knew. Deep down, she knew. They were all gone…

Ansley scanned the scene once more as if in a haze. The room was heavy with death and Ansley's despair. Bile rose in her throat, and she felt suddenly cold all over. As she turned, Ansley could see through the door she had left open to the world of green and yellow only a few feet away. She pondered how atrocities could exist so closely with such calmness. Ansley collapsed onto the old wooden floorboards next to her mother, and her mind retreated from the horror into welcoming darkness.

TWO

Ansley stood and looked outside the small window in her grandmother's house. The sun had not been up very long, and the kitchen air still had a bite to it. She tried to focus on her breathing as she watched her grandmother walking toward the front door. Her grandmother had spent the morning at the burial site for Ansley's family, negotiating a time for the funerals. Ansley had asked to stay home until it was absolutely necessary for her to go. She was thankful that her grandmother had taken over planning the service. Every time she began to even think about what had happened to her family, a large knot would obstruct her throat, making it impossible to breathe. She wasn't sure how she would face the rest of the day, but she knew that she had to. She owed her parents that much.

Ansley stepped away from the window and pulled a chair out from the kitchen table. The wood was worn and starting to show its age. She wondered how many times her parents had sat in these chairs. She could almost imagine her father sitting here as a young boy and arguing with his siblings. Ansley placed her hands on her face and tried, once again, to take deep breaths.

The door opened noisily as her grandmother entered. She said nothing, but came and placed her hand on Ansley's shoulder before going to her bedroom to have a few moments to herself. Ansley knew this was hard on her. She had not seen her grandmother react since she had initially told her what had happened.

Ansley had awoken not long after collapsing. When she was able to get herself together, she immediately grabbed her horse, Sal, and went over to her grandmother's cottage. She burst through the front door and startled the poor woman. She startled her even more when she shared the news.

The soldiers were sent for. They were the peace-keepers of the land. Most had been trained in Avendale, since it was the capital of Arvenia, but they hailed from towns and regions all over the continent. Ansley had urged her grandmother to wait to return to her parents' home until the soldiers had arrived, but Bianca had insisted on going alone. She told Ansley that it was important for her to see it for herself.

After Bianca had returned, Ansley noticed that her face was leached of color. Her cheeks were wet with tears, but she did not say anything to Ansley. She had simply sat at the kitchen table and let the tears fall until the soldiers arrived.

Ansley rose from the table. Her head was starting to pound, though she knew she had waited long enough. She went to the guest room, where she now had most of her clothes and belongings, and began dressing for the day.

***

Ansley fidgeted in her dress. She had decided on the black one. Her mother had sewn lace onto the sleeves and hem. Ansley remembered when her mother had made it for her. She'd asked "What is this?" when she'd seen the lace.

Leila had smiled wide and replied, "Lace! Everett picked up some in Avendale, and I wanted my girl to look beautiful!" Her mother had touched Ansley's cheek and added, "When it is done, you will see how the lace adds to the dress. You'll love it!" Ansley fidgeted again, trying to let go of the memory as the priest continued speaking.

She couldn't focus. The sun was shining, and she couldn't help but ask herself why it had to shine on such a horrible morning. She looked around, trying instead to appreciate the large group that had gathered. Of course, their neighbors were there, but others had come from Avendale and the far reaches of Terra. She wasn't surprised. Her father had been elected parish leader when Ansley was around seven or eight, so he was well known. She was surprised to see tears falling from several people. She hadn't known how her family had been cherished.

Ansley turned and looked at the row of caskets beside her. Four caskets. One for each person she loved so dearly. She choked back tears as she bowed her head towards the ground. *How could this have happened?*

When they had returned to her house, she and her grandmother had both sat as the soldiers inspected the broken home for clues. But only one had been found.

Besides the fact that her parents had aged well into their fifties in just a short amount of time, a small symbol had been drawn on the floor next to her father's body. It looked as if the killer had dipped his finger in her brother's blood. Ansley hadn't noticed it when she'd come inside. She was too distraught. The soldiers had been diligent in their search, and they had determined it must have some meaning.

Beside her father, almost tucked underneath his arm, was a circle with an arrow underneath it. None of the soldiers could guess what it might've meant, but upon seeing it, her grandmother had raised her eyebrows in surprise. She had not spoken to Ansley about its meaning, but Ansley knew that there was something she was not telling her.

Ansley was suddenly drawn back to reality by a small, warm hand placed on her shoulder. She turned to see familiar green eyes and a smiling face she knew well.

"Josilyn." Ansley said as she hugged her old friend. "Thank you for coming today." Ansley could barely stand to look her friend in the eye because of her grief. Josilyn sensed this and turned with Ansley to glance at the large group that had begun to mingle amongst one another.

"Ansley, I don't know what to say. I am so *sorry*. Nobody deserves this kind of death. Your parents were so full of life and brought such joy to the parish. I'm sure we will all feel lost without them." Ansley could see Josilyn watching her out of the corner of her eye. Josilyn's long golden hair blew in the soft breeze, framing her round face.

Her friend had always been tall and thin. Her blond hair was a rarity in Terra, and Josilyn was easily envied by all the girls her age. Luckily, she also possessed something much rarer: a kind heart.

Ansley and Josilyn had met as young ones in the parish. They had spent many years growing and exploring together. When Josilyn's family moved to another cottage, it became difficult for the girls to stay close. They had always checked in on each other, but they rarely had the opportunity to spend time together like they used to. Ansley never realized how much she had missed Josilyn's company until that moment. Her friend helped shrink the lump in Ansley's throat, making it easier for her to breathe.

"I found them. Did you know?" Ansley asked softly, glancing at her worn black shoes.

Josilyn merely shook her head, eyes wide. She reached out and placed a hand on Ansley's arm.

"They were in a puddle of my brothers' blood, but it was wrong, Josilyn. My parents had...*changed.*"

"What do you mean?" Josilyn asked. A crease settled between her eyebrows.

"They were *old*. My father seemed like an old man, and my mother's hair was dark grey. The weirdest part was that my father and mother had no wounds. How could they have died if they had no wounds?" Fury rose in Ansley's chest.

"I don't know. I've heard of people poisoning others with a draught or oils. Perhaps this was the case for them?" Josilyn offered. She quieted as several of Ansley's neighbors approached and nodded their condolences before turning to leave.

"Maybe, but it was definitely odd. There has to be something I'm missing. I do think it must have been done by dreamwalkers. Have you heard the reports from the other parts of Arvenia?" Ansley asked her friend.

"Yes. There have been attacks. Many have died, but it never mentions strange conditions like those you saw with your family. But I guess it wouldn't with the typicals being the ones that usually find the families. They don't know we exist." Josilyn replied.

Ansley nodded. Confusion still plagued her, but her thoughts were interrupted by her grandmother.

"It was a nice service, don't you agree?" Nana said as she strode towards the girls with a soft smile on her face. Ansley couldn't help but notice the dark circles under her grandmother's bright, blue eyes. Neither of them had gotten much rest.

"It was, Nana, but I think I'd like to go and rest. Will you walk with me?"

"Of course, Starlight," Nana said as she gave her granddaughter a comforting hug around her shoulders. "It's good to see you again, Josilyn. I haven't seen you since your inheritance ceremony. How have you been?"

"It's been an adjustment, but I think I'm finally mastering my skill. I never guessed that I would be a shifter since it's not a common skill in my family line. When I first thought of the idea of shifting in dreams into someone or something new, it worried me at first. Now, I almost look forward to changing," Josilyn said as if telling a secret. "But please, don't let me keep you. I'll check on you later, Ansley." She nodded a farewell to her friend.

Bianca turned towards her granddaughter and took her by the hand before steering her towards her home. The sun slowly fell below the horizon. It was going to be a dark night. There would be no moon, and being out past nightfall was unwise with the recent events.

"It's good to see you two together again. You used to be inseparable!" Bianca said in a cheery voice, but Ansley couldn't help but notice the emptiness of her grandmother's eyes as she spoke.

"Yes, she was my best friend. Josilyn was always up for my schemes," Ansley said, smiling despite her mood. "But she's been more distant since her ceremony. I hope that we can spend more time together once I inherit." Ansley glanced ahead to watch Josilyn join her tribe on a horse-drawn cart, probably headed to the east side of Terra.

Once a dreamwalker inherited, they were required to join a tribe for protection. The law had been followed for thousands of years. Long enough for everyone to forget where it had come from. However, dreamwalkers' bringing their abilities to a tribe was a tradition that had its benefits. It took more than just one walker to fulfill the missions handed down to them by the elders. Josilyn had found her place amongst her fellow tribe members easily enough, and she seemed to be blossoming into a strong dreamwalker.

"We need to talk about that. With everything happening, I think it may be the best time for your ceremony, Ansley. The only way I can protect you now is to give you your skill and teach you to use it. I fear if we wait longer, you will only be more vulnerable."

"What does that mean? Do you think they will come for me?" Ansley asked softly, her eyes shifting in the direction of her parents' home.

"I don't know, but we must arm ourselves with any weapons we have available." Nana looked at her earnestly. "I know you are grieving just as I am.

Unfortunately, time is moving quickly, and we have no extra time to spend with our feelings. When you are safe, we will grieve, but now is the time to act. We know that your family looks down on us from the stars, so we must move forward knowing that they would want us to do so."

Ansley nodded as the knot returned to her throat. "So, when should we do it? Have the elders given you a date?"

"Not yet. I am hoping to speak with them tomorrow. We will make our plans after the meeting." Bianca kissed Ansley on the forehead and began walking briskly across the field. Ansley followed, hoping her grandmother had left plenty of firewood inside to warm them against the cold memories stirring in the dark night.

THREE

Six years earlier

Ansley and her brother sat in front of her father. Ansley was only twelve, and she and Ryker had decided they were not going to bed. Leila had failed in encouraging them. In spite of her attempts, they had started a chant and decided that they wouldn't rest until their requests were met. "Sto-ry. STO-RY. STOOOOO-RRRYYYYYYY!" The walls echoed with the requests of the two children.

Their father laughed so loudly that the walls shook, and his blue eyes glistened playfully. "Very well! Which one will you have?"

"Father! Tell the one about the monsters!" Ryker demanded. At three years old, he barely reached his father's knees, but that didn't keep him from making demands of the burly man.

"No!" Ansley had protested. "Tell about Stellos!"

"Stellos it is!" Everett had agreed. He had always loved the story himself, and he didn't ever need much convincing to tell it again. He leaned back in his chair to begin his tale as his children settled in Leila's lap.

The Birth of the Dreamwalkers

Vito and Orco had always been at odds. Vito, the father and God of Life, sought to create. His brother Orco, the God of Death and Destruction, sought only to destroy.

Vito formed the world with his hands and took pride in watching over his creation. His wife, Matrisa, asked if they could make humans to serve as their children. She was a loving god and sought only to share this great love with others. So, being a dutiful husband, Vito gave in to the wishes of Matrisa.

Matrisa loved her children and asked Sali to bless them. Sali, the God of Earth blessed them with all manner of living things to tend to, including animals. In the darkness, Orco sought to destroy them all.

Afraid of direct battle, Orco found that it was best to attack the people at night while they rested. Many succumbed to him, forfeiting their lives. This continued for a millennium before Matrisa approached Vito.

"Husband, my children are dying. We must help them." She said earnestly.

Vito appointed Kius, God of Night, to solve the problem. Kius, being already tasked with pulling the moon across the sky each night, wanted a fast solution. He asked Matrisa to choose a man to help him protect the people. Matrisa had always favored Stellos. He was hard-working and toiled daily on his farm to help provide for his family. So, the Great Mother approached him. Stellos heartily agreed, not knowing what any of this would mean, for he was just a man.

Kius took his monthly break from pulling the moon across the sky to meet Stellos. He again asked if the man was up to the task of protecting the people from Orco. Stellos again agreed, and Kius placed his hand upon Stellos's forehead. In this moment, Stellos's forehead glowed with the four symbols of the dreamwalkers. Kius had gifted him with the ability to enter into the people's dreams. Stellos could persuade, see the future, wield the elements, and shift into any form to protect the people.

"We shall call you, Walker of Dreams. Go, and do your duty." Thus, dreamwalkers were made. Stellos took happily to his task, but he was still only a man. The gods had forgotten that men have limits where gods do not.

Orco attacked Stellos every night, and he slowly wore down the man's resolve. Though Stellos had been gifted with the power to form water, air, and earth in the spiritual plane of dreams, Stellos could do nothing to prevent Orco from whispering in his wife's ear while she slept. Once she awoke, Eva told Stellos that the gods had been selfish, asking him to take on their own responsibilities. She encouraged Stellos to rise up and challenge them, for he must be god himself if he had such power.

Years passed, and Stellos's contentment faded. Each night he battled, and each night Orco whispered lies to set Stellos against the gods.

Finally, Stellos had enough. He waited and plotted for his rise. When night fell, Stellos ventured to look for the gods. He caught them unaware and murdered many of their children. Kius and Vito banded together and withdrew Stellos's powers. With the help of Poeno, God of Justice and Punishment, the two gods banished Stellos from the earth into Orco's care.

Unsure about the fate of the people, Matrisa again approached the pair, "But my children! Their dreams will never be safe from Orco!" So, Kius and Vito decided that men were too easily swayed to have such an array of skills. To prevent a rebellion in the future, Vito chose to separate the powers forever, never to be connected inside a single dreamwalker again. He placed his hands over the world to spread them amongst the people.

"Wait!" Kius urged. He whispered into the god's ear to ask that a fifth power be added to ensure the dreamwalkers had a secret weapon against Orco, and Vito nodded in agreement. Again, the god stretched his hands over the world and let the powers find their places amongst the people. They multiplied and found their ways into thousands to prevent the weakness of one dreamwalker from overcoming the gods' purposes for these talents.

"Now, our children are safe. The shifters, seers, and persuaders will keep the wielders at bay. Whenever Orco tries to rise, they will hold back his efforts against the people," Vito said to his wife.

Thus, dreamwalkers were separated from typicals and brought into existence.

***

Present Day

The council of elders of Terra paced in front of Bianca. She had finally been approved to meet with them. Bianca had never considered herself special, and the elders certainly didn't make accommodations for her visit today. Each parish had their own set of elders, but Terra's elders were the head elders for Arvenia. Their parish had been chosen to house the head elders for two reasons. First, they were the parish with the largest number of dreamwalkers. Second, their parish was most central in the country. Bianca had always considered her elders to be very wise and level-headed. Nevertheless, they were disturbed by the news she had brought to them today.

"This has not happened for hundreds of years!" Quinn exclaimed. Her brown eyes widened behind golden-rimmed spectacles, and wrinkles seemed to overwhelm her forehead. The woman was much older than Bianca, but dreamwalking had kept her fairly young. Her face had only begun to show age once she had passed her skill onto a young one in her family. At that time, Quinn had been elected an elder on the council and taken over preserving the precious history of the dreamwalkers.

"I stressed the importance, to Ansley, of performing the ceremony as soon as possible. It is essential for her protection." Bianca replied with a sigh, worry emanating from her frown.

"But that will leave you vulnerable as well. You know that once the ceremony is started, your skill will be gone. Don't you think it will leave you more vulnerable if there is another attack?" Alden asked. He stroked his short grey beard as he peered at Bianca from under the glasses hanging onto the end of his long nose. His white hair reflected the number of years he had lived without a skill, but it also boasted his wisdom. He had led the council of elders for over 10 years, and his approach was always one of caution.

"It may, but I see no other option. We must protect her. *She* is vulnerable. I believe that her family was targeted. If I am right, they will come looking for Ansley next. Besides, I have lived my life, and she has only begun hers. Giving her the protection of a skill will ensure that she has a chance to do the same." Bianca replied desperately. She was unhappy with how the council was responding only to the threat and not to who it was directed towards. *Couldn't they see that Ansley was in danger? Did anything matter at this point other than protecting the girl?*

"I think Bianca is right," Daro said solemnly. He stood from his seat at the table and walked towards Alden, his older brother. Daro's hair was still brown, unlike his brother's, but it did not mark him as naive. He had only been elected a member of the council the past year, but his wisdom had already helped them avoid unnecessary dangers with the typicals. "Bianca should perform the inheritance ceremony. We need Ansley prepared if disaster should strike twice."

"Then so be it. Perform the ceremony but keep us informed about what skill she gains. I'm not sure why our foes have now come out of the shadows, but it seems they have a plan. It will be in our best interest to try to stay a few steps ahead of them this time." Alden murmured, obviously torn over his own decision.

"Our hope is placed rightly in Ansley. She will not fail the trials," Bianca declared earnestly as she bowed to her elders and turned to leave the room. Ansley *wouldn't fail. Bianca wouldn't allow it, even if she had to go into Ansley's trial and save the girl by herself.*

***

Bianca spent that night preparing for the ceremony as Ansley slept. She checked on her granddaughter frequently, but the girl never woke. She was sleeping a deep and dreamless sleep, which was for the best. Bianca was thankful that her sleeping draught had been successful. She placed the extra leaves from the shade of dreams into an empty pot, which she hid in the back of a kitchen cabinet. Bianca did not tell Ansley that she had added a small amount, ground finely to a powder, to her cup of wine. She had to ensure that Ansley would avoid dreamwalking tonight. The girl needed rest.

Bianca watched Ansley sleep as she leaned against the doorway to her guest room. It was so difficult, as a young one, to not move to the dream realm. Dreamwalkers grew more successful at using their skills with the passing of youth. She was happy to provide Ansley any rest that she could. She couldn't bear to imagine what the poor child had felt when she had stumbled upon that horrible scene in her home. When Bianca had gone to the house herself, she had been unable to look upon her son without dropping to her knees. Everett had been one of seven children who had blessed her life and made her a mother.

Bianca was proud of all that her children had accomplished, but she had cherished Everett the most. Sadie had moved to Avendale to escape farm life. Joseph and Jackson had retreated to Westfall by the sea to train and join the soldiers. They had always wanted adventure. Stephen, Margaret, and her husband had all died over thirty years ago. A disease outbreak had passed throughout the nation of Arvenia. When it hit Terra, it was devastating. The disease caused a high fever and could result in death. Margaret had been seven, and Stephen was only three. Her husband, Edwin, had been forty-six.

Ryker, her son whom poor young Ryker had been named for, had traveled across the sea in hopes of starting a new life away from his heritage. Unfortunately, Everett had been closest with Ryker and had missed him terribly when he left. Everett had been only ten when his oldest brother vanished and couldn't yet understand why Ryker abandoned his family. Bianca felt that Everett had developed a deep compassion for Ryker over the years, which breeded understanding as well. He had never spoken of his brother after he had married Leila. Bianca had always worried that it was a source of deep pain for her son.

Bianca continued to reflect upon her family as the night passed in silence. She was not emotionally ready for the ceremony but knew that it was Ansley's time. So, when the sun set on the next day, they would begin.

Bianca sighed as she filled her basket with the necessary items for the ceremony: candles, a knife, an old satin scarf, and a bowl of lavender. She sat the basket near the door, and she blew out the candles in the kitchen as she retreated to her own room for some much needed rest.

FOUR

Ansley felt as though every crunch of grass filled up the heavy silence of the night. She had been following her grandmother for almost an hour on a lightly-worn path through the Dream Hollow Mountains. The sky was darkening as the sun fell to the west. With the sunlight disappearing, all elements of comfort in the mountains disappeared. They were replaced by dark silhouettes and sounds of hungry animals. Ansley was careful to stay close to her grandmother. She touched the bow she had hung over her shoulder in reassurance against the dark night. Her pulse slowed in response to the comforting presence.

Bianca held a lantern to light their way and traveled slowly ahead of Ansley to avoid the roots and rocks that might trip them. Her grandmother had insisted on the ceremony taking place tonight, and she had also insisted that it be kept a secret. Ansley was not sure why. Ceremonies were usually a highly celebrated event. Only the two that were participating in the ceremony were allowed inside the ceremonial location, but the family of the new dreamwalker would usually host a celebration at their home. The celebration would happen at the same time as the inheritance ceremony, and it would continue until the trials had been completed. Eventually, the new dreamwalker would rejoin their family in the celebration. Some celebrations lasted up to a week. Ansley had never felt this was essential for her own ceremony. Still, she had at least expected to invite her close friends to celebrate with her after the trials. She understood the need for haste but mourned the idea she had always had of what her own ceremony would look like. Her *whole* life was starting to feel so different from the idea she had for it.

As her thoughts wandered, Ansley hiked after her grandmother through the woods. Their path had just started to grow steep with more trees and less rocks, so she knew they must be close to their destination. Ceremony locations were chosen by each family line. The families had used the same locations for centuries, and she had always known her family's was in these mountains. You were not invited to the secret location until your own ceremony. Dreamwalker ceremonies were public, yes, but young ones were not allowed to watch them. This was to protect the privacy of the ritual. If a young one was to observe the proceedings before his or her own ceremony, there was a chance they might use the knowledge to try to steal skills for themselves. Her father had always said, "Youth is cherished, but it is often absent of wisdom."

Ansley reflected on this for a moment, knowing that for most families the stealing of skills was not a concern. However, her family had experienced this only a few decades earlier. She was thankful not to have witnessed that tragedy and considered it lucky that her family had even survived. They had rebuilt themselves and continued on.

Ansley spotted a small, man-made cave built into a stone wall. The darkness made it look like an ominous entry to another world, and she supposed that's exactly what it was. An entrance to her future.

Her grandmother made for the wide opening, which Ansley noticed was covered with an old wooden door. The door was painted black. As they drew nearer, Ansley could pick out distinct shapes of a design.

Amongst the old and peeling black paint, stars were painted all over the door, much like the sky they traveled under tonight. The stars were all different sizes. Ansley realized they had been carved into the wood. Her family crest was at the center. She took a deep breath in as she gazed on it for the first time. Like the ceremony itself, a family's crest and name were kept secret from all who had not inherited. The stars in the crest all fell into a pattern of a constellation. *The Bear!* Her father had always pointed out this constellation in the night sky. She smiled at the memory and moved closer to the door. Each star had a marking in the center. She reached out and brushed her fingertips against one. They were single markings, but they seemed very distinct. She looked toward her grand-mother in question.

"Those are our names," Her grandmother smiled in reply. "Before we leave, you may have the chance to mark a new one for yourself. These are the names of all of our family that has come before you. All of the dreamwalkers who passed those skills on that you will now inherit. They watch over us from the stars." She whispered and raised her eyes towards the sky. Ansley thought back on their conversation from after the funeral when her grandmother had made the same comment. She smiled at all the subtle hints she had been given throughout her childhood towards who she was. Bianca touched one finger to her lips and then to her forehead in salute of those who were no longer with them. When her grandmother looked back at Ansley, she had a small smile of pride on her lips.

Her grandmother opened the door and gestured for Ansley to enter. Ansley took a deep breath and stepped over the threshold. She gathered her courage and tried to prepare herself for whatever may happen inside. The air was musty, and she coughed after enter-ing. She could only imagine how long this door had re-mained closed.

Bianca shut the door behind her and lit a few candles that she placed in rusted candle holders around the room. The holders stood at the level of Bianca's shoulder and lit the room enough for Ansley to look around. She noticed that the floor was marker with straight lines between each holder, forming a large pentagram. Two chairs faced one another in the middle of the shape, and this was where her grandmother had motioned for her to sit.

Ansley took her place in a worn chair and tried to calm her nerves. Her grandmother put the basket she had been carrying on the floor and removed a knife and a bowl of lavender. Setting these on the small table next to the empty chair, she reached back in the basket for what looked like a dark, navy scarf. Bianca laid it in Ansley's lap and continued her work. Ansley looked down and ran her fingers over the satin scarf. She had never seen it before, but she could tell it was very old. There was a faded design. She brought it closer to her face to examine the fabric. Tiny silver stars were sewn over the satin. The scarf itself still seemed as if it were new. She presumed it was only used for these ceremonies by her family.

"That was your great-great-grandfather's. He was the first to suggest a scarf. Before that, they used a rope," Nana stated with a crooked smile. She began grinding the lavender in the small bowl.

Ansley felt her face grow warm, and she crumpled the scarf in her fist.

"Easy, Starlight. It is just you and me here." Her grandmother said with a steadying voice. "Do you trust me?" She asked while looking sincerely at her granddaughter.

"Of course, Nana." Ansley said softly but confidently. She released her tight grip on the scarf and tried to distract herself by glancing around the room again. The pattern on the outside of the door continued around the inside of the small cave. Stars lined the walls and ceiling with those similar but distinct markings in the centers. A bear made from hundreds of stars was on the wall across from her . It covered the wall from ceiling to floor, and despite her nerves, Ansley felt that the constellation gave her courage.

"Alright. I believe we are ready," Bianca finally said as she settled into the chair facing Ansley. Ansley snapped out of her reverie. Her grandmother moved the table in between them and placed her bowl of lavender in the middle. She lit another candle that she had removed from the basket, used the flame to light the end of a bundle of lavender, and placed the candle in the center of the bowl. The room filled with a pleasant and soothing aroma. Ansley relaxed into her chair, thinking only of her mother.

"The herbs are only to help you relax. The process is more difficult if you are unable to sleep," Bianca explained. "Now, give me your hand." She reached across the table for Ansley, and Ansley placed her right hand in her grandmother's. Ansley's senses were alive. She noticed each passing second and every tiny movement of her grandmother's hands. Bianca looked up at Ansley with a small smile. She must have realized that not only were Ansley's hands freezing, but they were also shaking. The corners of Bianca's eyes crinkled. "Are you ready, child?" She asked Ansley.

Ansley only offered a nod, since her heart was stuck somewhere in her throat. She swallowed hard and made herself look into her grandmother's brilliantly blue eyes. Bianca laid the burning lavender into the bowl next to the candle.

"I, Bianca of House Black, acquired, used, and now I freely pass on. My skill belongs to my family." She said as she used her knife to cut a single small line across her palm. She held her hand palm up as she reached for Ansley's hand again.

"Repeat after me: I, Ansley of House Black, now acquire. My family's skills are now my own." Ansley repeated the words, barely hearing herself over the thundering of her heart. Her grandmother cut an identical line across her palm. She marveled at the gentleness of her grandmother's hand and was thankful for the kind, loving woman who sat across from her. Her grandmother then moved swiftly, placing her hand on top of Ansley's and using her left hand to bind their hands together with the scarf. Bianca leaned forward until her forehead touched Ansley's and closed her eyes. Ansley closed her eyes and waited.

She suddenly felt a burning on her forehead where her grandmother's face touched her own. The moments passed silently.

When Ansley opened her eyes, she found herself somewhere new. She blinked tears away in the bright light. Her hand reached up instinctively toward her face to shield it from the sun.

She had made it. Now came the trials.

***

Bianca leaned back, breathing deeply. She felt as though someone had kicked her hard in the stomach. Her granddaughter still sat facing her with her eyes closed. Bianca gently unwound the scarf from their hands and stood. She was weak. Her knees trembled as she moved closer to Ansley. She lifted her granddaughter from the chair and gently laid her on the cot along the wall. She could not go with her on this part of her journey. She would have to wait for Ansley to return. In the meantime, she needed to rest and regain her strength.

Bianca tried to push aside the thought that Ansley may fail in the trials. It was uncommon but did happen for some. Bianca had such faith in her granddaughter's destiny to become a dreamwalker. She remembered having a conversation with Ansley's parents only a few months ago. They had all shared the same thoughts. Ansley would easily master the trials. If she did emerge unsuccessful, Bianca would find another person for Ansley to inherit from. Multiple attempts were allowed but not suggested. Skills were numbered, and the elders generally discouraged wasting them on a second attempt at the trials, which would likely end in failure.

Bianca sighed. She reached up to her forehead and traced the fading outline of an inverted triangle with a single line passing vertically through it, marking her as a wielder of earth. Once so familiar to her, and now never again to appear. She remembered when she had first emerged and felt her mark. Her family had been so proud. Another wielder of earth. She tried to walk back to her chair and stumbled, falling heavily on her knees. Bianca cried out sharply from the pain and eased herself on her side. She lay there for several minutes before trying to rise again.

Her skill was gone. She couldn't deny that now. The emptiness she felt confirmed it. She only hoped that Ansley would survive her trials and return to her quickly.

Bianca closed her eyes to welcome rest while Ansley began her journey.

FIVE

The sun beat down, warming Ansley's bare feet. She stumbled forward after walking up a particularly large dune, landing with her hands in the hot sand. Her feet were unsure on this terrain. She had never lived or even traveled anywhere outside of Terra. It felt like she was on another planet.

Her mouth felt dry and grainy from the sand blowing in the wind. She wasn't sure how long she had been here, but it felt like hours had passed. She tried to recall how she had gotten to the dunes, but the memory wouldn't come to her.

Ansley kept walking but was not quite sure where she was going. The entire landscape was sand dunes. She began to lose hope of ever finding her way out of this place. Her mind sought desperately for a solution to this extreme heat, but her thoughts grew foggier by the minute. She seemed to be moving in slow motion and thinking even slower. Where was she anyway?

Then a thought struck her. This was a dream. Ridiculous, but it had to be true. She had never seen a place like this anywhere near Terra, so it had to have been made by a wielder of earth. She stumbled along, gently urging herself to remember how she had come here. An image came to her. She remembered her grandmother sitting in a chair and speaking to her. Nana had cut her hand and placed it on Ansley's, wrapping it in the silk scarf. Could she be in her trial?

Ansley had given a lot of thought to what dreamwalker trials would consist of, but it had never occurred to her that it would be a physical test. Ansley lifted her hand to wipe the sweat from her forehead. Her lips felt like dried paper, and her tongue felt leaden in her mouth. Moments ticked by. She turned in search of anything out on the horizon, but she was searching in vain. It seemed that the sun, the sand, and the sky were her only companions on this journey.

During her training, her father had told her that the trials would determine if she would become a dreamwalker. If she failed, she would survive, but most young ones who failed were preyed upon by others after their ceremony. The majority of dreamwalkers were good hearted and cared for other dreamwalkers and typicals, but there were those that abused their skills. Ansley tried not to dwell on the possibility of returning to that fate.

She shivered, seemingly impossible in this heat, as she remembered another conversation she had with her father. He had spoken of the Asps family boy who had gotten lost in the dream realm during his ceremony. The boy had never found his way back, and his family could not find him either. His body had lived on, but his mind had not. Nobody knew what had become of his spirit. As tradition dictated, each dreamwalker faced their trial alone, so it was a mystery to the boy's family who or what had prevented his success. The family had mourned him as his body slowly died. Answers had never been found.

Ansley diverted her mind away from these troubling thoughts. She tried instead to take one step at a time and not tumble down the large dune she had spent so long climbing. It wasn't until she reached the top that she spotted a slow-moving river below her. It sparkled like thousands of jewels, as if welcoming her for a drink. She took careful steps down the side of the dune, but she eventually lost her footing. Ansley tumbled and rolled the last ten feet down, finally stopping near the rocks around the riverbed. She gasped for breath and hastily tried to remove as much sand from her eyes and mouth as possible. She hated this stuff. It had coated her entire body, making her feel like a giant, walking dust heap.

Returning her focus to the river and the surrounding land, she tried to determine if anyone else was here. It looked deserted, but she could never be sure in a dream. Dreamwalkers could hide their presence if they wanted. Skilled dreamwalkers could observe others night-after-night without that person ever knowing. Well, she felt that she had definitely given up on masking her own presence with that fall down the dune.

Ansley got to her feet and took a few wary steps toward the river. As she drew closer, she could feel a cool breeze blowing off the water. She knelt and cupped her hands. The water was a cool relief on her sunburnt skin. She lifted a small handful to her face and rinsed the remaining sand from her mouth. She continued to wash up for several minutes before finally deciding it was best to dunk herself below the refreshing current. When Ansley leaned up, water streaming down her face, she was startled to see someone standing silently beside her.

It was an old woman. She looked like she had lived for at least 90 years, but she did not appear feeble. Her white hair reached her waist, and her face was marred by wrinkles. But her eyes were a warm chocolate that glowed with kindness and youthfulness . The woman stood tall, and she loomed over where Ansley sat in the sand. The woman shook her head and opened her mouth to speak.

"You are wasting time. Get out of here! Find the door!" She shouted. To Ansley's surprise, the woman then leaned forward and placed her open palm on Ansley's forehead. Ansley immediately felt her skin burn beneath the woman's hand. She leapt back, only to find the woman had disappeared.

Dreamwalkers

Ansley tentatively touched her forehead as tears filled her eyes from the pain. She could feel what seemed like a brand in the middle of her brow. A small oval shaped brand. What had just happened?

Ansley turned back to the river and gasped in horror when she saw what laid below the surface. The clear water ran over thousands of bones. Skulls, femurs, fingers, and rib cages were submerged below the moving surface. Ansley gagged. She had just drank and washed with that water. She hurriedly backed away from the river and lost her footing. She stumbled over her feet as she tried to put distance between herself and the river. Suddenly, blood began to drip down between her eyebrows. Confused, she reached toward her brow again. The brand had been replaced by a cut. It was bleeding, and the flow only seemed to be growing heavier.

Ansley's confusion doubled as her emotions took over. The blood from her wound mingled with tears that now flowed freely down her cheeks. Find the door. Ansley had to get out of there, and she had to do it fast. The woman had warned her. Time was running out. Ansley scurried back toward the large dune that brought her to the river.

Her confusion grew as the minutes ticked by, and her anxiety increased tenfold. She could now feel her heartbeat in her brow as blood started to drench her shirt. Ansley stumbled along hopelessly, trying to

*drag herself up the dune towards where she had origi-
nally awakened. She didn't dare to look down and examine herself. The dune seemed immense, and Ansley
felt herself fatigue with each step. Finally, she sank to
her knees in the sand as the world around her grew
hazy. She reached out with her mind hoping to find the
answers she sought.*

Door. Find a door. *Maybe she was supposed to
build a door. Her family had been made up of wielders
after all. Wielders controlled an element in dreams,
usually earth, water, or air. Her grandmother had been
a wielder of earth, and it was likely that she would be
too. Ansley placed her palms down on the burning sand
and willed herself to feel a wooden surface. She closed
her eyes and pictured holding onto a door handle.
When she opened her eyes, the sand still slipped
through her fingertips. Frustrated, Ansley beat her fists
into the golden flecks. She gazed quietly for a moment
at the specks of blood that had fallen from her face.*

*She drew in a deep breath and told herself not
to cry. Panic was seeping in. She knew if she didn't find
the door soon, hers may be the next set of bones to settle
into that riverbed.*

*A sudden chill fell over Ansley. Though she
tried, her eyes would not focus. This must be what dying
felt like, she thought unhappily to herself. The feeling
intensified until her world turned black. Ansley blinked
but saw nothing, and her fear seemed to paralyze her.*

She reached out and found the ground again. Still sand. When her eyesight returned, she saw herself sitting in the sand. Ansley looked over her own form and toward the river again. She was drawn to a spot on the other side of the river. A small house sat on the far bank. Ansley's vision came back with a big gust of wind. She blinked the confusion away. How had she been looking down at herself?

Ansley took a deep breath and looked down at her hands. They were covered with blood. She had to act now. She stood quickly and turned back towards the river before setting off in an awkward run across the dunes. When she reached the riverbank, she leapt as far as she could.

It wasn't far enough. Ansley plunged into the now rapid current. She gulped air down before her head disappeared below the surface, and she started kicking her feet as hard as she could manage. Her head once again found the surface as her legs continued their hasty kicks, propelling her towards the other riverbank. Ansley's hands had just met the rich, brown soil when something tugged at her ankle. She turned and saw a hand tightly grasping her. The bones had come to life and were pulling her back into the fast-flowing current.

She kicked furiously but could not shake off the hand. It pulled and pulled, trying to bring her back below the surface. Ansley fought harder, yanking handfuls of grass along with her into the water. Finally, she jerked her foot and broke the hand free from its skeletal arm. Ansley threw herself from the river and crawled across the bank towards the small wooden house. She could still feel the hand tightly gripping her leg, but she kept her mind focused on her goal.

Ansley had just reached the door when a strange sound drew her attention back to the river. Her pursuer had also freed itself from the river and was crawling toward her. A skull stared at her through empty sockets, and its one remaining hand pushed the rickety set of bones upright on its feet. Hastily, she twisted the metal door handle and pushed the door in-ward. She entered into darkness and slammed the door tightly closed behind her.

***

Ansley sprang up from the small cot in the cave. She reached quickly toward her leg, making sure there was nothing attached to it before she turned her attention elsewhere. She sighed in relief when she found only her thin ankle bone. Her breathing slowed, and the panic began to subside. She looked around the room and spotted her grandmother on the floor nearby.

Bianca sat up and turned to her. "You have finally found your way back. I was worried because you were gone for a long time," she said as she struggled into a sitting position.

"What? How long have I been gone?" Ansley asked.

"Two nights," Bianca said as she looked over her granddaughter, inspecting her from head to foot. "Are you okay?"

"I don't know," Ansley whispered. She walked over to her grandmother and let herself collapse into her grandmother's strong arms. "It was horrible, Nana."

"It's over now," she murmured as she patted Ansley's back. Bianca pulled away to look at her granddaughter and gasped. She reached her hand toward Ansley's brow with a confused look on her face.

"What's wrong, Nana?" Ansley asked. She reached up and touched her own hand to her brow, finding the same mark she had felt in her dream. It was starting to fade away. She could barely make out the edges of the oval with her finger. "What is it?!" She exclaimed, looking in fear at her grandmother.

"It's your gift. We are all marked in our trials with our gifts. You have the eye, Starlight."

"The eye? What is that supposed to mean?" Ansley asked as she continued to gingerly touch the spot on her forehead. The skin returned to its normal texture, and the mark faded away under her fingertips.

"You are a seer," Nana whispered, her bright blue eyes wide with fear.

SIX

Ansley stared at her grandmother in confusion. "A seer? But I don't know anyone who is a seer. I didn't think they really existed…"

"They do, but usually there is only one per family. Seers are only gifted when needed. A family can go years without one. One typically does not emerge unless we need to see the future to protect ourselves," Nana replied. Her wrinkled forehead signaled the confusion she felt at Ansley's mark.

Ansley looked closely at her grandmother, but she had heard her say it. Seers were only gifted when *needed.* For *protection.*

"Nana, this is crazy! I can't be a seer!" Ansley shouted indignantly. "By gods! How am I supposed to protect anyone?" She stood and turned away from her grandmother in frustration. Her eyes drifted over the stars lining the cave walls. She was supposed to be a wielder, like her parents. Like her grandmother. Not something useless that could easily get her killed.

"Ansley, we can talk about all of this later, but right now, we need to get you back home. The elders will want to know as soon as possible about this turn of events," her grandmother stated as she reached for her empty basket and began blowing out the candles. Ansley noticed that the candles had almost burned completely out in her absence.

"What do you mean *turn of events*? Won't they be happy to have a seer?" Ansley added softly, fear still echoing through her words.

Her grandmother stepped slowly toward Ansley and grasped her granddaughter's face between her callused hands. "Yes, but that makes you even more vulnerable. You know that seers cannot protect themselves easily in dreams. That is why we have to get you out of here. I gave my skills over so that you could inherit yours. I can't protect you anymore." Nana released Ansley and turned back to the items in the cave.

"Here," she said as she handed Ansley the small knife they had used earlier. "Mark your star. You belong here now," she said, motioning toward the walls before turning back to packing up their gear.

Ansley looked dubiously at the knife in her hand. *How could this have happened?* She could only imagine what her parents would have thought of her new skill. To know that their daughter, the daughter of many generations of wielders, had been named as a seer. She picked a spot closest to the bear's jaws and carved her small star. *If I have to be weak, I could at least fool my descendants*, she thought bitterly. She drew her mark in the center of the star: an "A" with light beams flowing out from around it. Her father had called her Starlight, so this would be her design. She glanced at the wall. How many of the others had been gifted the eye? She sighed and turned back to her grandmother, dropping the knife in the now-full basket.

"Let's go," Nana said briskly. She pushed the old, wooden door open. Ansley took one step outside the door and heard her grandmother close it quietly behind her. When she turned back to Nana, her knees buckled. She fell to the ground immediately and felt herself drifting to sleep with no way to fight it.

"Ansley!" Her grandmother screamed in the darkness around her. She sounded so far away.

***

Ansley found herself in a small house, looking around the kitchen. A figure was moving by the stove.

"Hello…" she said as she reached toward who she now realized was a young woman. Startled, the woman turned to face Ansley. It was Josilyn.

"Ansley?" Confusion filled Josilyn's green eyes. "What are you doing here?" Her golden hair was pulled away from her face into a braid. Ansley thought it made her look like she was just a child again. Josilyn's green eyes shone, but no smile lit up her face.

"I don't know how I got here, Jos. I just…" Ansley trailed off as Josilyn suddenly disappeared. Ansley turned and looked around the kitchen in confusion. "Josilyn? Josilyn!"

Ansley turned in circles, screaming her friend's name as her vision became blurry again.

***

Ansley felt herself being jostled from the dream and awoke on the cold, damp grass. She took in the darkness around her and the glittering stars far above. Her grandmother's face swam into her sight as the cool, night wind blew across her face.

"...got to get up. Ansley, did you hear me? Stand up and see if you can walk." Nana tried uselessly to pull Ansley off the ground, but her arms seemed too weak. Ansley noticed that her grandmother's movements were slower than they had been.

"Nana, I think Josilyn is in trouble. We have to help her," she said, feeling the blood drain from her face. Her mind was clouded with the vision of Josilyn disappearing from thin air.

"Did you have a dreamvision?" Bianca asked, her blue eyes widening again in recognition of this strange new skill. "Come on. Let's get back to the house. We will go to her as soon as the sun rises."

Ansley allowed herself to be soothed for the moment, but she could not help but feel the after-effect of the ominous dream. Her knees shook as she followed her grandmother out of the Dream Hollow Mountains, and every step felt more difficult than the one before. She knew that their journey in had not been this difficult.

Her thoughts centered on Josilyn and Josilyn's horrified eyes when she disappeared. *What was happening to her?*

SEVEN

Rosalie
500 YEARS AGO, The Black Night

Rosalie took a look outside her small, glass-paned window, admiring the land around her cabin. The sun was starting to rise higher in the sky over the pines. All seemed peaceful, but the air was full of a tension that she could not shake. Her husband, Stephen, had just gone out to milk their cows, a chore he cherished doing each morning.

Rosalie was a petite woman. She had dark hair that she kept in a tight bun on the top of her head to keep from over-heating while working on the farm. Her chin was sharp, but she also had a smile that made her eyes sparkle. Stephen always told her that it was her smile that had won his heart.

She stepped over to the fireplace and stirred the pot of boiling stew. A delicious aroma rose from the broth, and she reached for a spoon to taste the flavors she had been working on for the past hour. *Maybe a bit more seasoning*, she thought as she reached for the stack of herbs that were stashed on a shelf above the fireplace. She lay the herbs on the table, grabbed a short knife, and quickly chopped some basil and an onion she had been saving. Then, she filled her hands with the ingredients and tossed them into her stew. It had been her mother's recipe, and she had always loved sharing her family's recipes with Stephen. He didn't care much for the lamb, but she knew that the meat was what gave flavor.

Terra was a pleasant place to live. Rosalie had enjoyed spending her first summer here. Harvest was quickly approaching, and she knew that they would have plenty of crops to reap. Stephen had invested in several types, but most of his funds went to corn. Shortly after they bought the farm, they learned that corn flourished in the soil in Terra. Stephen was willing to try other crops, but he wanted to plant what he knew would grow easily. Avendale was dependent on Terra's crops to help the people avoid famine. Likewise, Stephen and Rosalie were dependent on their own crops to fund their new life.

The people of Arvenia endured a horrible famine just five years before. The food had burned in the hot sun that summer, and there were limited crops to keep the people fed. Avendale had suffered the most. The capital of Arvenia was bustling, but the ground was hard and dry. It was unsuitable to grow anything to eat, and other parishes held onto their crops instead of selling them to the people in Avendale. It had been a disaster. Many had starved before King Deryn decreed that these lands be turned into farmlands.

To think a mountain girl like herself was now a citizen of Arvenia! Rosalie's mother would have been proud to know she had risen so far beyond her family's status. When these lands had been deemed farmlands, King Deryn had offered each acre at an incredibly low price. Stephen asked Rosalie to marry him and start a new life here in Terra. Now, she was a member of a parish, and her children and grandchildren would be raised on this land in the many years to come.

She shook the thought from her head and focused on making bread to accompany the stew. Her hands dug into the dough and began kneading and rolling, adding flour as she worked. Her thoughts drifted back to her life before the one she now knew.

The Dream Hollow Mountains had been her home, but life there was hard. Much harder than the one she had in Terra. Her family of eight had lived in a tiny cabin hidden amongst the pines. Her parents, the Galloways, were dreamwalkers, but that did not protect them from the dangers of mountain life. She remembered one evening when a wild panther had jumped on the roof of their modest house. They had heard it scream as it tried to claw its way inside. Thankfully, the panther gave up his attempts to break into her family's house after about an hour's time. Rosalie remembered sitting on the bed she shared with her five siblings. She had held her three baby sisters to keep them from crying. Her terror had been real. Rosalie sighed in relief as she glanced again out the window of her new home, thankful that wild animals didn't prowl this land.

She shaped the dough in a small pan and put it into the oven. Her flour-coated hands brushed off on her apron as she stood. Stephen would be back shortly, and she knew he would be ravenous after completing his chores. A loud crash made her jump. She pulled off her apron, set it aside, and began walking toward the door when it was thrown open. Stephen stepped through with a crazed look in his eyes.

"They are coming! We must hide!" He shouted as he grasped her by the arm and shoved her into the small closet they housed their quilts in. "Stay quiet," he whispered through the small cracks. She heard him move the table in front of the door to keep her presence a secret.

Rosalie's heart beat a rapid symphony. A recent dreamvision of hers came to mind, but she pushed the thoughts from her mind. *It can't be possible*, she tried to reassure herself. She tried to slow her breathing, but there was no use. She thought they would be safe so near the city of Avendale. It seemed they could never escape the terror that had been growing in the past few years. Even here in Terra, Rosalie had heard of the many dreamwalkers that had been disappearing all across the country. She had never imagined that she and Stephen were at risk.

Tears slipped down her face as she thought of Stephen out in the open, exposed. *He will not survive this!* It distressed her even more.

She tried to push that thought aside as she sank to the floor in the narrow space. A loud boom shook the cabin around her. She placed her shaking hand over her mouth to keep her sobs inside as tears poured down her face. All thoughts of her future disappeared as quickly as a candle being snuffed out. She listened to the defiant yells from her husband and said a prayer to Vito for him. The silence eventually swallowed all sounds of Stephen. She cried harder and closed her eyes to escape from the terror separated from her only by a thin wooden door.

EIGHT
Ansley

Ansley and Bianca stepped out of Josilyn's door and walked toward their horses that were tied near the barn. Josilyn waved happily as she stepped back inside her quaint new home. She lived miles away from Ansley's, so it had not been a quick ride.

"I *am* glad she is okay, but I just don't understand, Nana," Ansley said quietly. "If I am a seer, shouldn't my dreamvisions show what happens?"

"Ansley," Bianca replied softly, "It doesn't always work that way. This skill is new and may be different than you just seeing what is going to happen next." She reached out and patted her horse, Bill, on the nose as he chewed on a bit of hay. "You have to find your trigger before you can learn more about it. Your skill may be showing us the distant future."

Ansley grabbed Sal's saddle. As she pulled herself up, she shook her head. "What is a trigger? I've never heard you talk about that before." She frowned in confusion as she steered Sal away from the barn and toward her grandmother's house.

Bianca looked over at her granddaughter without answering. She swung herself slowly into Bill's saddle, indicating the strain it had placed on her back. She let out a deep breath.

"I never told you because I didn't think you would ever *need* to know it. Seers are not common in our family." Ansley looked over at her grandmother and noticed Bianca's frustration.

Ansley turned away from her grandmother to look west across the valley. She couldn't see it from here, but her family's house was ahead. Her family lived maybe eight miles from Josilyn's new home. *Had* lived, she mentally corrected herself. Ansley had not been back to the house since the funeral. She couldn't bring it upon herself to face everything the small cabin held. She had decided to stay with her grandmother instead. The Black house was locked, and her family's belongings remained there with the memories of their life together.

Ansley hadn't forgotten, but she knew that she had let the last few days distract her. She couldn't begin to imagine how her grandmother felt about everything. After burying her son and grandsons, she had given away the skill that had protected her for the last fifty years.

Ansley let the conversation end and steadied Sal as he trotted towards her temporary home. There would be time to master her skill. She didn't need to try to learn it all at once. The sun warmed her back as she pulled herself back to reality. She mentally began to prepare herself for the list of chores that waited for her when they arrived back at Nana's.

***

Quinn and Daro sat around Alden's kitchen table and listened to him read the letter they had just received from Bianca. It contained the results of Ansley's ceremony. Quinn leaned forward in her chair.

"This is not a good omen. The Blacks haven't had a seer in around 500 years! Does this mean our peace has ended?" The lines on her forehead seemed more pronounced as she awaited their responses. She fidgeted uneasily in her chair, and her glasses sat precariously on her nose.

"I agree that it is not a good sign, but we have prepared the best that we can. The families have been alerted and prepared since the first signs started a few months ago near Willow. All we can do now is wait. We will not know how to counter these forces until they attack again," Daro stated as he took a sip of his dark, steaming coffee. "Besides, many of the other dreamwalker lines have seers, and their emergence hasn't predicted any danger."

Alden laid the letter down and tapped his fingers on the table. He looked up at the map that was stretched above his fireplace. Stars marked the settlements of all the dreamwalker families under his guidance in Terra. There were four families in the area: the Blacks, Asps, Mannes, and Brooks. Each family was marked by their own distinct constellation. To the west and south of the great city were the Scouts. To the east of Terra were the Fischers on the coast. *So many families that could be victimized.* But, Daro was right. They had all been informed of the dangers they faced. They were in the gods' hands now. He said a silent prayer to Matrisa, mother and peacemaker of the gods, and stood from the table. He walked slowly over to the window, the gravity of the situation weighing heavily on him.

"We must wait. But that doesn't mean we are helpless. Send a messenger out to retrieve Damon of the Asps. He is experienced, and she will need what training he can provide." He turned to look across the rolling hills. "Bianca will keep us updated on Ansley's dreamvisions, and we will stay one step ahead of them."

***

"A trigger is something that pulls you into a dreamvision," Bianca explained to Ansley as she spooned some seasoned chicken onto her plate. Their discussion from earlier had finally been revisited, after Ansley's endless questions drove Bianca to finally share what she knew. She handed the spoon to her granddaughter and raised her eyes to determine the impact her statement had just made.

Ansley stared at the spoon without making a move. Bianca tried to keep her facial expression neutral, but in all honesty, she was concerned for the girl. A huge mantel had been passed onto Ansley, and she was still just a child. She wasn't sure if Ansley quite understood the responsibility that came with her new skill, but she would try her best to ease the girl into the concept.

Ansley sighed as she finally reached for the spoon and served herself dinner. Her hands shook slightly from the effort, arms sore from the extra chores she had done today. She had spent the afternoon at her parents' farm, tending to the horses and cattle. She had also checked on the cornfields to ensure they had not been plundered. Ansley had asked one of her old neighbors, Grady, to do the work for the vegetables and crops, but she preferred tending to the animals each day. Bianca had tried to refuse Ansley's help with her own animals, but Ansley had insisted.

"So, wielders, shifters, and persuaders don't trigger? Why do seers do it? I just don't understand, Nana," Ansley sighed again, taking a bite of the chicken. Her fork dug into the baked potatoes and sliced vegetables next.

"Wielders and shifters don't trigger. That's why I don't know much to help you. I was never taught the intricacies myself, but persuaders do trigger. Just like seers," Bianca responded, trying to avoid overwhelming Ansley.

"Why didn't I know this before?" Ansley demanded. "I feel like this is something Father should have told me."

"It is not usually shared until training," Bianca replied softly. "We only train those who are successful with the trials."

"What is the big deal, Nana?" Ansley raised her hands into the air. "Why is there so much hesitancy about telling young ones things like that? I feel like we will all know eventually!" Bianca grimaced. She was not doing as well at the *easing Ansley into the concept* as she had initially thought. She sighed and took a sip of her coffee. Black with one spoonful of sugar. Strong with a little sweetness to take off the sting. Similar to the way she had tried to teach lessons to her children and grandchildren.

"Ansley, would you rather us put ourselves in danger? You don't understand it now, but with time, you will grasp why the elders made the laws. It is all in your best interest."

"Fine. Keep your secrets, but at some point, you will have to share them." Ansley rolled her eyes and looked back to her half-empty plate. "So, what kind of triggers are there anyway and why do persuaders trigger?"

"Persuaders trigger on people in a different way. They can usually sense the people who are open to their power of persuasion and those who are not. Seers can trigger with anything. A smell, a touch, a feeling. The most common is a touch, of course, which is what almost all persuaders trigger from. It is more difficult to determine a trigger for seers. The actual events that are portrayed in dreamvisions can happen at the moment the dream occurs, the day before, or even years before. It's a mysterious thing that we have not had much opportunity to study or learn about."

"Why?" Ansley asked, seemingly disinterested in the response at this point.

"Well, persuaders are usually rare, and seers are often even rarer than persuaders. One family line will only have a persuader or a seer every several decades or longer. However, it is important to learn your trigger. We must start a dream journal for you each time you have a vision, and it will help us determine what is leading you to them."

"And when we find out? What do we do then?" Ansley inquired. Bianca noted the desperation in her granddaughter's voice. It reminded her of when the girl had been a small child trying to learn her lessons for school.

"We wait. Wait for you to be triggered. It is likely that once we know it, we can also try to trigger you to help us learn of the outcome of upcoming events. That could help us protect tribes and families."

"Right. Protect our family…" Ansley murmured to herself. She took her plate to the sink and rinsed off the residue of her meal.

Bianca bit back another explanation as she sensed her granddaughter's exasperation. "Ansley, how are you doing with all of this?"

Ansley's back was turned, but Bianca could feel the tension. "Nana, I just wanted it to be easy. Why couldn't I have been like father, mother, or you?" Bianca heard a sniffle, so she stood and walked to her granddaughter. She pulled Ansley into one of her best, bone-crushing hugs and tried her best to squeeze the sorrow out of her.

"My dear, you may be a seer, but none of us can predict the path that life will lead us on. There is very rarely a straight or even easy journey to the finish line. The rocks and roots along the way, whether big or small, help us to prepare for the mountains up ahead. Sometimes, they even help us prepare others for the rocks that will be in their paths, too." She looked at Ansley and brushed a tear away from her tan cheek that had grown red and hot with emotion.

Bianca released Ansley with a kiss on the head. The child had already had enough to think about at the moment. Bianca grabbed her own plate from the table and cleaned it before retiring to her rocking chair on the porch. Once she was sitting comfortably, she pulled a sealed letter from her pocket. She read the update from the council of elders. The letter fell from her fingers. *They had sent for Damon? What were they thinking?*

***

Ansley tossed and turned on her soft pillow and murmured to herself as she slept…

She walked down the hill to her parents' home, pulling Sal's reins to steer him towards the barn. She heard a gasp and picked up her pace before running towards the sound. Grady was on the hay-strewn floor of the barn with his hands covering his chest, fingers spread wide attempting to keep the blood inside of himself. "Get out!" he screamed at Ansley, as he pointed to the door.

Ansley ran to him, dropping Sal's reins. Sal, now spooked, took off in the direction of Bianca's farm. "What happened? Grady, are you okay?" Blood bubbled up around his lips. She noticed that the injury on his chest was from a pitchfork, with multiple wounds piercing him in a line.

Ansley applied pressure like her mother had taught her to do many times after her father had sustained injuries while tending to his land and cattle. Panic flooded her senses. The blood oozed out around her fingers. She couldn't help but cry out as her friend let out a big breath of air. He hadn't even had time to respond to her question before his eyes turned glassy. Ansley stared at his face in shock, feeling terrified and suddenly cold from the biting wind blowing through the barn. She reached to close his eyes, accidentally smearing blood over his entire face.

Ansley stood from Grady's lifeless body and held her arms out in front of her in horror. She was covered in his blood. She let out a wail as she pushed her way outside of the barn doors to fresh air…

***

Ansley awoke with a start. The horrible scene that had just unfurled in her dream still flashed before her eyes. Her eyes shot down to her arms, but there were no signs of any blood on her. She threw the covers back and ran down the hall to her grandmother's room.

"Nana!" She whispered fervently as she shook her grandmother by the shoulder to wake her. Bianca's eyes flew open, and she murmured sleepily, "Good heavens, Starlight! What is it?"

"I think I had another dreamvision! Get up! We have to go to my farm. Quickly," Ansley ran out of her grandmother's room and grabbed her thick coat off the nail in the kitchen. She hurried out to the stables and readied Sal and Bill, placing heavy saddles on their backs. They didn't seem too appreciative of being disturbed at this hour either.

She was just walking them around the front of the house as her grandmother stepped outside in her coat and thick black ankle boots. She had swept her hair into a modest gray bun on the back of her head. Ansley helped her grandmother into Bill's saddle and noted the time it took her. *That is fairly new*, she thought to herself. Bianca was very capable for her age, but Ansley had noticed lately that she was taking more effort to do everyday activities that had once been easy for her.

Ansley pushed the thought aside and climbed into her own saddle. She took off at a gallop towards her family's farm. Tendrils of light grew on the horizon. She had not noticed the time. It must've been dawn.

She took in the scenery around her and breathed in the freshness of the air coming off the mountains to the northeast. Neither would calm her racing heart. The mountains stood in the distance like a formidable ally, blocking the sun and providing the shelter of darkness she needed to cross the rolling hills. They arrived as the light began pouring ruby reds and brilliant oranges across the sky.

Ansley looked away from the house, fighting the memories that surged, and turned back to the old, weathered barn. What once brought forth calm and comfort now made her shake. She dismounted quickly and quietly as she moved closer to the source of her distress.

Her grandmother moved behind her almost as silently as a ghost. Ansley realized that she had not even told her grandmother what had happened in the dreamvision. She shook her head in frustration at her stupidity in leading an old woman to the sight of a murder. She raised her hand to stop her grandmother and turned to face her.

"Wait in the house. I will go look and report back to you." Bianca shook her head silently and pointed to the closed barn door with a question in her eyes.

"Yes, in there. Can you let me handle this?" Ansley asked in an almost silent whisper. Her grandmother did not say a word, but the look on her face drew a reluctant sigh from Ansley. "Fine, but let's tend to the horses first."

Ansley watched as her grandmother tied Bill's reins to the only tree providing shade to her family home. When she had finished and rejoined Ansley, they turned and began to quietly creep towards the barn. Ansley was disturbed when she heard a noise coming from inside. She turned back to Bianca and touched her finger to her lips to indicate silence. She reached out and took the leather handle into her hand and pulled it slowly open. With the door open, Ansley sprang inside expecting to see a bloody scene before her.

Instead, she saw Grady standing there with a pitchfork, mucking out the stall for her father's horse, Abe. Ansley frowned in confusion. Grady looked up from his work.

"Ansley? What are you doing here so early?"

"I thought you were in danger. I just came to make sure you were okay."

"What? How would you even know I was here? I know you said you'd handle the animals, but this is the least I could do after everything your father did for me. Besides, the baby started crying, so I couldn't sleep anyway." Grady used the sleeve of his shirt to push back the damp hair that had fallen into his eyes.

He had always been a kind man. He and his wife had moved into their small cabin last winter to begin preparing for their first child and summer of raising crops for Avendale. He was not a dreamwalker, so Ansley's family had always tried to keep them unaware of their gifts.

Ansley's grandmother stepped into view. "Oh hello, Mrs. Bianca," Grady said, smiling in her direction. He turned back to Ansley. "Really, what is this about?"

"I just had a feeling…" Ansley began, "Well, it looks like you're alright, so I'll get inside and try to scramble us up some brea.." as she began to finish her sentence, rough hands grabbed her by the shoulders and shoved her into the hay. Ansley screamed. She rolled out of the hay onto her hands and knees and tried to trip her assailant by grabbing the man's feet, before he moved too close to Grady. Unfortunately, her attempt didn't work. He advanced on Bianca.

The old woman faced her assailant head-on, but she didn't have much fight in her. She threw a punch that only found empty air before the man grabbed her by the shoulders and threw her onto the hard dirt floor of the barn. When she fell, Ansley heard her head hit the floor, and she saw blood trickling down her grandmother's forehead. Bianca lay still with her eyes closed. Ansley glanced up at Grady and shared a look of terror and determination.

Then, Ansley sprang forward as the attacker now moved towards Grady, who had shifted his pitchfork in the direction of the invader. Ansley jumped on the man's back, trying to pull him to the ground. Her small arms were no match for the man's bulk. He laughed in response to her attempts and threw Ansley to the floor once more with little effort. Turning away from Grady to look down at her, the man shook his head sadly.

"You are pathetic," he said just as Grady brought the wooden handle of the pitchfork down on the man's head. The man tumbled to the ground, unconscious. Grady ran to the back of the barn to get a small rope. He grabbed the man's limp arms and tied his hands with thick knots. Grady shifted the man's heavy weight onto a small milking chair that Ansley dragged over from the corner of the barn.

After Grady began securing the man to the chair, Ansley ran to her grandmother. She was just beginning to come to, and the blood was clotting in her hair. "Are you okay, Nana?" Ansley asked softly, helping her rise to a sitting position.

Bianca merely grumbled as she reached a hand gingerly to her brow. Her eyes found Grady, who was finishing up the touches on the rope around the unknown man's feet. "We need to alert the council, Ansley." She said in a gravelly voice.

Ansley nodded and turned to Grady.

"Grady, will you send a messenger for Alden Black? He has been helping us investigate the attacks on my parents. Nana and I will wait here with him," she said, gesturing to the stranger, "until they arrive."

"Of course. I will," he replied and laid his hand on Ansley's shoulder with a concerning look on his face. "I'm glad you had a feeling that you needed to come over this morning. You may have kept me alive, Ansley." Grady walked out of the barn towards his own home to retrieve his horse. She knew he would ride for Alden himself even though she had suggested a messenger. Ansley sat down in the hay opposite their attacker. She shook her head in disbelief. Then, she pulled on her coat to shield herself from the chill in the morning air.

NINE

Kenna

The sun fell quickly on the eastern coast of Arvenia. Pleasant sounds of the sea filled the small community of Willow, and families drifted from the docked boats to their homes to begin preparing dinner. Kenna locked the door to her small store and closed the curtains. The floor to ceiling windows gave her the perfect view of the shimmering Glass Sea. She had always loved this time of the day, when the sun began to fall below the horizon. The salty air drifted in along the breeze. Kenna closed her eyes to breathe in the familiar scent of her home.

Kenna was tall and of medium build. Her brown hair fell down past her shoulders and illuminated her usually animated face. She wore a simple linen shirt and tightly fitted pants that were tucked into leather work boots. Nothing about her wardrobe was extravagant. Still, there was always something striking about her appearance.

Kenna pulled her bag onto her shoulder and gave the sea one more glance before turning down the road that would take her home. Her heart filled with such peace as she inhaled that last salty breath of air for the day. She sighed deeply and turned away from her old friend.

It had been a steady day at work. Kenna owned a small general store on the harbor that offered a variety of goods to the people in town and those docking at the harbor. Fresh fish, salted meats, fresh vegetables, canned and preserved foods, fabric for clothing, personal items, and even candy for the little ones who liked to pop into her store. She had recently purchased an icebox to hold homemade ice cream but had yet to find the time to set it up. Kenna knew it would draw many more of the fishermen's children into the store in the afternoons. She smiled to herself as she thought about the child who had accompanied his mother today. He had nearly climbed the counter to get a good look at all the glass jars of candies she had to choose from.

Kenna rounded a corner and came to her building. The housing in Willow was primarily built off the dock to prevent flood damage. Most of Willow's people lived in buildings that were several stories tall, with the first levels left unoccupied. It had been a long time since the last storm that bred flooding, but it never hurt to prepare for the worst. Each building could house many different families in homes known as flats. Kenna assumed it was called this because each family had only a single level of space to live in.

Edric and Kenna had enjoyed moving into their flat a few months after they had married. It had only been two months, and Kenna loved coming home to him each day. They were still considered "newlyweds" in the community. They had tried to make the flat their own. Kenna added pots of her favorite flowers and plants to the windowsills, specifically lavender and geraniums. Edric had commissioned an artist to paint Kenna and his family crests, and these hung side-by-side over their large couch. Being born as a Fischer, Kenna's crest was made of stars in the shape of a fish. Edric's was a rearing stallion. Kenna always found it interesting that Edric's crest was one of a land animal, when he preferred the sea. But then again, she had never met Edric's family, so she didn't know if they shared his love of the ocean.

She entered the building and climbed two flights of stairs to her flat. As she neared the door, Kenna thought about Edric's family. He had told her they were wealthy and had not supported Edric's decision to leave them. He had made his own way after moving to Arvenia, and Kenna couldn't have been prouder to call the hard-working man her husband. She opened the door and found a very different scene than the one on the harbor. Her husband was preparing dinner. She stood in the doorway and took in the sight with a grin. Several pots were on the stove, each simmering with some delightful aromas. Edric was leaning down from his towering height to take something out of the oven. His head dipped below the counter as Kenna stepped closer to greet him. He stood and placed the hot pan on top of the stove. A delicious aroma emanated from the dish.

"Hello there, darling!" He roared before turned around to wash his hands in the sink. His handsome face lit up with a smile, and Kenna remembered the first time they had met. He had stepped into her shop, fresh off a ship, eager to find something hot to eat. She had directed him to the nearest inn, not expecting herself to get lost in his eyes. He was from Calvenia, to the northwest of Arvenia. Edric had a foreign look about him. His hair was dark, and his body was lean. He was also almost two heads taller than Kenna. Everything about him was dark, except for his eyes. They were green like her own, but Edric's were light. Almost like Kenna's favorite type of apple.

"How was your day?" Kenna asked as she gave Edric a quick kiss on the lips before walking to the stove to help him finish cooking their meal.

"We got a full load of tuna, whitefish, and snappers today, but we had to come in early. The storms were drifting in, and the captain was worried we would get caught out in it. Suited me just fine. I like being here when you get home," Edric said with a devilish look in his eye. He reached out quickly and caught Kenna in his arms. He pulled her in for a tight hug and then leaned back to survey his wife. "More beautiful every day," he whispered, slowly pushing her hair away from her cheek. She kissed him deeply, enjoying the familiarity and comfort of his embrace.

After they pulled away from one another, Kenna helped Edric finish the meal: lemon seasoned fish with potatoes and herbs. Being married to a fisherman and running a store on the dock meant fish for most meals.. They enjoyed their dinner before settling down by the fire. Kenna picked up the monthly local flier that updated the parish on important events. She gasped at the headline.

LOCAL FAMILY OF SIX FOUND MURDERED

"Yes. I saw that too. Don't seem so surprised though. This has been happening for weeks, Kenna," Edric said as he looked up from his book. "This family was attacked a few weeks ago and barely escaped last time. They were lucky that the neighbors heard them screaming for help. It's obvious that these attackers had marked them for some reason."

"The *whole* family, though? Even the children? Edric…I can't imagine." Kenna looked sadly at her husband before touching him on the arm. "There has to be a reason for this."

"We shouldn't assume that the victims were dreamwalkers."

"Why shouldn't we? They were Fischers, and all the dreamwalkers on this side of the coast share that name. It has to be so!" Kenna said exasperatedly.

"You aren't a Fischer," Edric said glancing, at Kenna. Her eyes flashed in response. He quickly added, "Let's try not to think about it tonight. This is only the second time this has happened in our area, babe."

"But Edric! It may only be the second time here, but it has happened other places too. I have read the fliers brought in by the captains. It is happening in Inverness, Wusylla, Terra, and even as far as Westfall. If it isn't stopped, these murderers will just continue to wreak havoc."

Edric stood from his chair and moved toward Kenna. She gasped as she continued reading. "Did you see this part? The children were killed with weapons, and the parents were not marked. It says here that they seemed to have aged over 30 years since the last time they were seen…" Edric took the flier from her hands and folded it. After laying it on the table, Edric pulled his wife to her feet and gave her a hug.

"Kenna, you have always been drawn to helping others, but some things are not for us to worry about. We cannot resolve this horrible wrong. Let's go to bed." He kissed her on the lips and smoothed her hair back behind her ear before leading her into their bedroom.

Kenna did not say anything else about the flier that night, but she knew something had to be done. She couldn't help but think that the people who were concerned, like herself, were all being quieted by their loved ones or their fear. *Staying quiet will only allow the culprits more time to carry out their attacks. By the time someone finally decided to take action, it would be too late.*

Kenna pursed her lips in the dark room as she listened to Edric's soft breathing. Images of those four innocent children occupied her thoughts. She turned onto her side to find a more comfortable position, but sleep continued to evade her.

I won't wait. I can't. I am going to do something even if nobody else will. These thoughts seemed to ease her mind into resting. She let out a deep breath, releasing the tension from her shoulders for the first time since reading the flier. When morning came, she would make her plan.

TEN
Ansley

By the time Alden had arrived, his glasses askew and an air of panic about him, the strange man had awoken. Ansley found his presence daunting. He sat calmly while he surveyed each of his captors with heavy lidded brown eyes. He kept his secrets to himself, though Ansley, Bianca, and Grady had not attempted to bring those secrets out.

Ansley hovered near the door, Bianca seated next to her on a hay bale. She was holding a soft cloth to her head. The bleeding had started again when Bianca had moved from the floor, so Ansley ran to the house to find something to quell it. Her grandmother had remained uncharacteristically quiet, but she kept her keen eyes focused on the enemy before her. Grady had returned with Alden in tow. Both men were quiet as they settled their horses in the barn to rest.

When Alden finally approached the pair, Ansley turned to face the head elder of Terra, noting the intimidation she suddenly felt in his presence. He seemed to notice this too, and he softened his look and said, "No need to tell me what happened here. Grady caught me up on the ride." Unspoken words flashed from his eyes as he glanced in the direction of her family friend. Ansley nodded and turned to Grady.

"Grady, I think we've got it from here. Thank you again for retrieving Alden."

Grady nodded but didn't hide the concern on his face. "Of course, Ansley. Can I send for the soldiers for you too?"

Alden took over now. "We will send for them as soon as we have let the horses rest." Grady turned to look in Alden's direction, who was merely another old man to him. He nodded in resignation, and lines of exhaustion appeared on his forehead.

"I'll leave you to it then. Let us know if you need anything else. Ansley, please don't worry with the animals here. I will tend to them too. I know you have so much to shoulder at the moment," he said, fighting off a yawn.

"Thank you, Grady. Sleep well," Ansley replied as she watched her kind neighbor walk out the door and back to his own innocent family.

Alden turned after Grady had exited the barn and set his sights on the strangely quiet man tied to the chair. The man met his glare with a ferocity that would make any man tremble. Alden's glare was hot enough to set the barn on fire, but the man did not seem phased.

Ansley, sensing that she was not needed, retreated to where her grandmother sat nursing her wound.

"Who *are* you, and why are you here?" Alden growled, rattling the tin roof of the cozy barn. The man was unaffected and even smiled in his interrogator's direction without answering.

Several minutes passed. The silence was unnerving. Ansley stole a glance at her grandmother, who seemed to radiate the fear that Ansley was also feeling. Bianca's face turned white, and she pursed her lips, as if trying to keep her feelings from exploding out of her. Ansley felt her hands begin to shake as she watched the fear and anger play over her grandmother's face. Alden took a step closer and grabbed the handles of the chair the man sat in; his face turned red with anger.

"What. Do. You. *Want*." The bite in Alden's tone rattled Ansley's bones, but her grandmother simply kept her eyes focused on the scene unfolding in front of them, her face still drawn and lips pressed tightly together. The man smiled and then let out deep throaty laugh. He turned his eyes to Ansley, and she felt the blood rush from her face.

"Twice. You were lucky twice, but I think your luck has run out," he said. Ansley swallowed. Alden grabbed the man's chin to redirect his attention. He growled another question at the intruder, but Ansley did not hear it. The man's words echoed in her ears. *Twice....Twice. Twice?*

"You killed them, didn't you?" She almost didn't recognize her own voice. It was so weak and tired, barely registering to her own ears.

The man laughed again. "I wasn't alone, but I did have the *honor*." His eyes glistened maliciously, and Ansley felt unable to move. Her movements became slow and effortful as anger built inside of her and grew like hot lava in a volcano. Slowly, it seemed to boil out of her nose and ears, leaving her face burning with anger. Suddenly, she was on her feet, walking to the man. He kept talking.

"You see, we needed to keep them alive until we could steal their skills. After that, they were only empty shells. Useless and disposable." Ansley's hands trembled with anger as she inched closer. It was as if it were only her and this evil man in the room, connected by the events that brought them together. She willed herself to not attack him for his crimes. He kept talking.

"But the boys, they were another story. I tasted their blood." His eyes glistened with madness, and he smiled a wicked smile in her direction. Ansley stopped moving as the horror set in. A vision of sweet Eli and Ryker chasing one another for a scrap of toast brought tears to her eyes, and Ansley felt her throat tighten as if someone meant to strangle her. She closed her eyes to keep the tears at bay. *They were just children! Why had they been subjected to such evil?* A loud noise prompted her to open her eyes once more. Alden must have punched the man. A small drop of blood clung to his bottom lip as he smiled manically once more. His madness continued.

"Orco's eye will rise again! Vito's dreamwalkers will fall, and the typicals will know victory! Your kind will regret the work you've spent your lives doing!" He hissed before using his tongue to roll something around in his mouth.

Bianca stood quickly and said, "No!" Alden turned to look at her, but that was all the man needed. He chewed up the leaf. His laughing soon turned to coughing. Blood spurted from his lips. In seconds, his body fell limp once more. His eyes stared at the ceiling, away from the destruction he had just caused.

"Nightshade," Bianca mumbled quietly to the silent barn.

Alden let out a string of curses before kicking the man's chair backward onto the floor. The intruder fell but uttered no sound.

ELEVEN

Ansley freed her hair from her braid and brushed it with her fingers. She wasn't ready to sleep, but she still pulled the covers back from the bed and climbed in. The horrors realized in her parents' barn seemed to follow her everywhere. She couldn't shake the images of that evil man killing her sweet brothers.

Everything he said had brought up only more questions for Ansley. *Why was he talking about Orco? Who was he working for? Why was he targeting dreamwalkers?* The last one was the most disturbing. It popped into her mind when Alden had excused himself from the barn to return to the rest of the council. *What aren't they telling me?*

Nana had appeared equally confused, but she insisted on both of them resting before doing anything else. Ansley had been too emotionally drained to refuse.

She sighed deeply and leaned back on her pillow. How long could this go on? She felt like they were making no progress towards finding answers, and she felt even more vulnerable. Her eyes fluttered close. She may as well rest while she could. She drifted to sleep before she could reach up to put out the candle…

***

Ansley found herself outside in her mother's garden. She smiled as she turned round and round to look at the flowers and vegetables. Taking her time, Ansley began to weave her way through the rows. She stopped and inspected plants, watered them, and picked foods from the vines.

She felt such peace, and she wasn't surprised when she turned and saw her mother leaning over the pumpkin patch behind her. Her mother's face was covered by the brim of her straw work hat, and her apron kept the dirt from her dress. After tending to the vine, she stood and began rubbing the dirt from her hands. She looked up and noticed Ansley watching her.

"Well don't just stand there like a weed! Come help me with this one! It's ready to be picked," she laughed and motioned for Ansley to join her. Ansley smiled and took a step in her direction. Then, her dream changed. Her mother was no longer with her, and her garden had transformed into a new garden. It looked like one in a large city, with row after row of beautiful flowers. People began walking on the path all around her, and children made loud exclamations while pointing at the beautiful display.

Ansley turned away from them with a heavy heart. Her mother was gone. Even in her dreams, she couldn't keep her for long. Ansley walked to a nearby wooden bench and sat, feeling sorry for herself. She looked around at all the families walking as a tear moistened her cheek. She reached up to wipe it away and noticed a stranger staring at her.

He was a young man, maybe only four to five years older than herself, and he carried himself easily. He was walking slowly in her direction. When he saw that he had caught her eye, he flashed her one of the most brilliant smiles she had ever seen. His bright blue eyes glistened, and his thick black hair was tossed gently by the soft breeze. He wore a simple white work shirt with the sleeves rolled up to his elbows. He didn't look like he belonged here in the city, but then again, she didn't either.

Ansley turned to look behind her, but nobody was there. The man was definitely heading in her direction. She sat quite still and tried to decide if she had ever met him. No memory came to her, so she assumed it was some dream person she had imagined.

He took his time walking to her, and he stopped by an especially large flowerbed to pick a cheerful daisy. He turned and continued walking until he could hold the daisy out to Ansley.

She looked up at him in sheer amazement. What was he doing? She shook her head and laughed. "I'm sorry, sir. You must have me mistaken with someone else," she said, still taking the daisy.

He smiled in response, never dropping those brilliantly blue eyes. "No, Ansley. I've been waiting for you, and you finally found me."

Even more puzzled now, Ansley asked, "Who are you? And how do you know my name?"

The man gestured to the bench beside her, and she nodded in reply. He sat down beside her and looked out to the massive garden. "My name is Rhys. I have seen our lives, Ansley, and you are at the center of mine."

"What?" Ansley asked, now a bit frightened. This odd situation was escalating quickly.

He turned back to look at her again. "I am a seer. Just like you." Then he reached over and touched her cheek gently, easing her messy black locks away from her eyes. "You aren't alone anymore."

***

At his touch, Ansley sat straight up in her bed. She looked around her bedroom to find her candle still burning, now very low, and everything else as she had left it. She tried to calm herself and settled back down on her pillow.

There were no other seers she knew who lived in Arvenia except Damon, whom her grandmother had been discussing earlier. He lived across the sea in exile and would not be returning any time soon. Was this a trick, or was her mind just playing games with her? Maybe her exhaustion was starting to take a real toll. She must've needed rest more than she realized.

Ansley shook her head lightly to dispel the image of Rhys's face. He was quite handsome, even if he wasn't real. She smiled to herself at the thought. She had never dated or been in a relationship with anyone before. It was nice to think that someone could cherish her so much, even if they weren't real. Oh well. Dreams were just dreams, right?

She closed her eyes as a big yawn escaped her mouth, drifting off again in search of Rhys. He may not have been real, but he could be a nice distraction.

TWELVE
Bianca

Bianca opened the door to her small home and watched as the council members passed through her doorway. She greeted Damon with a frown when he followed slowly after them into her kitchen. Bianca shut the door behind her guests and turned to accompany them to the dining room table. Ansley was out visiting Josilyn but would be returning shortly. She was glad her grandchild was not around to greet their visitors just yet.

The events of the last week had left Bianca's thoughts reeling. She had to admit to herself that she couldn't understand the motivations of the stranger who had killed her family, but she also couldn't mask the fear she felt in knowing that someone was still after Ansley. She had warned her granddaughter after that night to keep a low profile, but the girl was young. She doubted that Ansley even grasped what that actually meant.

Bianca took her usual seat at the table and gestured for the others to sit as well. Quinn sat on her right and Alden on her left. Bianca glanced in his direction, but he didn't acknowledge her. It was strange to see him so composed after the incident in the barn. After the man had died, Alden had left and sent another dreamwalker to help with the burial. The council leader had been eerily silent on the subject since then. Bianca couldn't shake the feeling that he knew more than he was choosing to share.

Daro chose to sit at the head of the table while Damon remained standing. She smirked in his direction. "Well, it seems you must always defy us, Damon, whether we are offering a helping hand or a seat."

Damon continued examining his fingernails as he responded. "Bianca, it seems you haven't lost your tendency to speak your mind in all situations, even if that means offending everyone along the way." He raised his dark brown eyes to glower at her. "Aren't I here to help *your* granddaughter after all? You should show some respect."

Bianca grasped the table edge tightly. Her temper had been short since last week. She simply glared in Damon's direction and tried to remain pleasant. He was right. She did need his help, and he was the only one who could train Ansley to protect herself.

"Can we get started?" Quinn offered in her hesitant way. She glanced between the four others and laid her stack of papers out on the table. Not only was she the historian of the council, Quinn was also the interpreter. The interpreter was in charge of reviewing dreams and delving out responsibilities to local dreamwalkers. Quinn's duties were usually considered happy ones, but not today. They also involved pairing new dreamwalkers with trainers.

"We do have a lot to discuss before the girl returns," she finished, glancing in Damon's direction.

Damon rolled his eyes as he pulled up a chair to plop himself into. His shaggy black hair had grown down over his ears, and his chin was covered in gray stubble. *Unkempt.* Bianca thought in disgust. It added to his overall rebellious personality and increased the frustration and repulsion she already felt for the man. She hated even more to think that he looked younger than her. She remembered first asking her own father who Damon was when she was only six years old.

"Tell me everything," Damon said as he looked up at Bianca with a grin that he knew would set her off. "I have been…*out of touch* for a while."

***

Ansley opened the door to her grandmother's house as she picked the twigs out of her long black hair. Nana had practically thrown her out that morning, insisting that she needed to get away from all this tragedy. Without a set plan, she had steered Sal in the direction of Josilyn's house in search of comfort and distraction.

The two girls had enjoyed their time together and shared memories just like they had years before. The time seemed to pass before she was ready. Josilyn had been initially surprised to see Ansley, but they quickly fell into old routines: gossiping and giggling over coffee.

When they had discovered what a beautiful day it had become, Ansley suggested a ride so they could enjoy the fine sunshine. She had never expected Josilyn to take *that* route on their ride, but Josilyn always liked her tricks. She shook her head with a smirk as she recalled her friend's laugh. She had been thrown off Sal's saddle when he had taken her through low-hanging brambles. Her chuckles died in her throat as she looked into the kitchen and found her grandmother sitting at the table with the Terran dreamwalker elders and a strange man.

They looked up as she approached. Ansley couldn't help but feel afraid of the man. He stared at her from under long, black hair that hung almost to his chin. His whiskers were gray, but he seemed to be just a few years older than herself. He slouched in his chair and picked his nails with a knife. *Was he a mountain man or something?*

Ansley moved inside the door as she continued to examine this stranger. His cloak was heavy and had a few snags that showed its age. He had a dark look about his eyes that conveyed his unhappiness at being here, and those almost black eyes seemed to pierce through her very bones. Ansley tore her eyes away from the man as she turned to drop her bag on the chair nearest to her.

"Ansley, we've been expecting you," Bianca said calmly.

"And who exactly is...we?" Ansley said, not trying to keep the confusion from her voice. She glanced in the direction of the man once again before pulling a chair out to sit in.

The man looked at her as he sipped from his coffee mug. It, unlike her grandmother's, was not steaming. Ansley suspected that it was something much stronger than coffee. There was no grimacing that usually followed sips of such drinks, but Ansley deduced that he must've drank freely.

"This is Damon. He has traveled a long way to meet you. He arrived a few hours earlier and spoke with the council while we waited for you to return."

Damon...The name stirred recognition. She looked over the man again and gasped as she noted the deep, red scars around his wrists. *Damon.* The very one her grandmother had been speaking about a few days ago. He was supposedly the only seer any of the families had emerge in the last 100 years. He had lived amongst the dreamwalkers for only a few years after his inheritance ceremony before he was exiled from Terra. News of his betrayal had been widely circulated, and she remembered her own father telling her about it when she was starting her training. He had committed unspeakable crimes against the dreamwalkers.

Ansley tried to moisten her tongue enough to offer a nicety. Damon seemed to sense this and spoke up before she had the opportunity. "Don't bother wasting your time, girl. We have little of it, and we should spend what time we have getting started."

Ansley glanced nervously towards her grandmother who gave her no explanation. Her heart thundered once again inside her chest. *What exactly were they starting?*

"What do you mean?" She managed to squeak softly, hating her voice for its betrayal.

"Your elders sent for me to train you. Seems they had use for a traitor after all," Damon said with a smile before taking a long draught from his cup. "Seers are hard to come by. We are the only two left in the country. If you are to be trained, it will be by me."

"Whatever you think you can teach me is better wasted on *someone else*. I can manage on my own," Ansley said lifting her chin a few inches.

"You may think yourself brave for those words, girl, but bravery or not, you are a *child*. You have no idea what you hold within you. If you'd prefer to navigate it yourself, that is your choice." Damon made to rise from his chair, and a loud squeak echoed throughout the room as the legs slid across the stones. Ansley looked up and saw her grandmother reach out quickly, placing her small, wrinkled hand on his arm. There was hopelessness in Nana's eyes.

"Please, Damon. You know we need you. Ansley meant no harm. She is just frightened. *Please!* Stay…" she pleaded.

"I am not, Nana. If I am frightened of anything, it is of *him*. How could you let a *traitor* into your home? Father would…"

"Don't *presume* to tell me what your father would do!" Nana boomed across the table. Ansley sunk back down into her chair in shock. Her grandmother had never raised her voice in such desperation and frustration. She quieted for a moment.

"Your father would be ashamed of the way you speak to guests in my home, Ansley. Wanted or not, this man is here to *help* you. You are an adult now, so you will swallow whatever pride you think you have and listen to what he has to say." Her grandmother's eyes blazed with fury as those last few words echoed in the kitchen. The council members found other places to devote their attentions.

Damon, still standing at the table, reached for his cup to finish his drink. "I will not stay where I am unwanted. It was only for the council that I returned in hopes of…mending old bridges." He moved away from the table as if to head towards the door. Bianca looked expectantly at Ansley.

"Wait!" Ansley saw Damon pause as his hand grasped the handle to the door. "If you are here to teach, then I will listen." Ansley said as she moved around the table towards the wild man. She held out her hand towards him. "I offer my apologies."

Damon looked down at her hand. He didn't take it. He only spat on the floor near her feet. "To hell with your apologies. I don't need or want them. You can keep those and any other comments to yourself. I require five days of your precious time, and then I will be gone. Whether you use what I teach you or not is your choice."

Ansley tried not to balk at his rudeness, though she remembered she had started this. She sighed before lowering her hand. "Five days it is, then."

Three days later

"You have to find your trigger. It is the key to understanding your visions and inviting them to happen," Damon said once again to Ansley. Damon had said this to her so much in the last 72 hours that she was starting to hear it when she tried to sleep at night. He looked much different than he had two days ago. His long hair had been cut to a short style above his ears and was wavy. His stubble had been shaved and left a smooth face that now revealed his youth. He had explained to her the day before that seers can live longer than most dreamwalkers. He was actually 92 years old, but his looks and youth had remained. He seemed no closer to the grave than herself.

"I know, but how do I *do* that?" Ansley asked frustratedly. No matter how many times he said it, it never made it easier for her to find her trigger. He was lucky. His was so simple. Sage. He would burn it and instantly be sent into a dreamvision. Damon had explained in detail that there were many different triggers, and they were as important as the visions themselves. They still had no idea how intricate her skill would be. She had discovered that not only could the trigger vary, but the visions could also be anything.

Most seers had visions of a specific type. Damon had revealed that his were of people's secrets. After discussing her first two visions, Damon had guessed the meaning of Ansley's. It wasn't pleasant.

"Yours may follow death. You are seeing the deaths of those you trigger for. This is a very valuable skill, Ansley. You could not only see death, but you may be able to prevent it as well," Damon had said, a light gleaming in those unfathomably black eyes.

Ansley had let the words sink in over the past day as she followed Damon into his visions. She had held his words deep inside and wondered if she had her skill sooner, could she have helped her family? She never spoke those words aloud. They swum around her head, echoing and sending pain into every breath she drew in. Ansley tried to push these thoughts away as she brought herself back to reality. She looked around at the trees that shaded her from the noon-day sun.

Damon had insisted on training her only in daylight. He brought her out early before dawn each day into the mountains, and then they started. After just three days, Ansley already felt more knowledgeable. She was surprised at how appreciative she was of the training and how comfortable she now felt in Damon's presence.

"Shall we go back?" Damon asked Ansley as he lit the small bundle of sage that he had laid on top of a flat boulder.

"Yes. I'm ready." Ansley said. She swallowed nervously, knowing that unpleasantly, now-familiar pull that she felt each time they went into a dreamvision together was imminent. Damon moved to sit by her and cut his hand with a small blade he had pulled from his boot. This had seemed so disturbing to Ansley at first, but Damon had quickly explained that this was how other dreamwalkers bind themselves to one another. All those who were in tribes or had training mixed blood. It gave them free access to each other's dreams. Damon had taught her this in his first lesson mere minutes before dragging her into his dreamvision. Now, the process had become second nature to her.

He handed the blade to Ansley, who swiftly cut across her own hand. Another red line next to the cuts she had made yesterday and the day before that. Ansley held the blade and her hand out to Damon so he could take her palm. Their blood mixed, and she leaned back against the large tree trunk.

***

Ansley opened her eyes and immediately spotted Damon up ahead. They were in a small village market. She walked slowly in his direction. He turned and smiled as he spotted her from behind the horses that were being led across the street. He then returned his attention to finding the source of his vision, and she noticed that his body grew stiff. He reached for the hilt of the sword he kept on his left hip.

The horses moved again, and Ansley's view became obstructed. She tried to move around them but was unsuccessful. Dreams could seem harmless, but the situation could quickly become dangerous if a dreamwalker was not careful. Damon had warned her many times of dreamwalkers who attacked other dreamwalkers in the last few days.

Upon running past the horses, Ansley was shocked at what she saw. Damon was on his knees with his own sword hilt protruding from his chest. Blood gushed from the wound, and he gaped up at his assailant as his breath caught in his throat. The man spat on Damon before turning to the men lingering behind him. They laughed as they walked away from Ansley's dying mentor. Damon looked at Ansley as she rushed toward him. Sorrow and pain filled his eyes, and she never had a chance to reach him.

***

Ansley's head cleared as her eyes sprung open from Damon's rough shake at her shoulder. She sat up and looked him over. Seeing that he was not injured and realizing that it was only a dream, she sighed in relief.

"Well, that was an unpleasant surprise," Damon said, looking at Ansley closely.

"What happened?" She asked in confusion. "I thought you were dead."

"I was. Don't you get it? That was your vision, not mine. You saw my death," Damon murmured as he reached towards his pack holding his flask. "I wish *I* hadn't. It seemed rather….unpleasant." He undid the stopper and took a long drink from the near-empty flask. Wiping his mouth with his arm, he handed it to Ansley. She was surprised by his offer but accepted it cautiously. She took a small sip and coughed violently as the liquid burned down her throat and settled near where she imagined her heart was.

Damon continued to examine her. "That could have been days or years from now. It seems your visions are a bit unpredictable, but it does help to know what they look and feel like. The only trigger that seems to be connected with your visions is touch."

"Touch? What do you mean?" She coughed again, trying to rid herself of the burn in her chest.

"*Touch.* Some seers are triggered by touching those who are in their visions. The sage has never triggered you before. All of the people you have had visions of are people you have probably shared a touch with at some point. A hug, a handshake, whatever.

116

Your friend and your neighbor. Now me. You had never had a vision of me before we first touched hands two days ago, had you?"

"No. Is that a *good* thing? To have touch as a trigger?" She looked down at her hands that now seemed to hold so much power. She ripped a small piece of fabric from her shirt's hem to stop the blood flowing from the cut she had forgotten on her hand.

"It isn't the best. It just means that we won't be able to *bring on* your visions. They will happen on their own, and you will have to act quickly if you wish to use them to change the fates of the people you see. Their *deaths*, I mean." Damon glanced again at Ansley, and she sensed he was concealing his true thoughts. She also thought she saw fear in his eyes.

"Come. Let's go back and rest for the day. I don't think any more training would be helpful after that vision." He stood from the soft carpet of grass and reached his hand out towards Ansley. She took it and was pulled to her feet. While putting out the fire on the rock, Damon added, "You will need to find a tribe quickly. You are going to need more protection than we had thought."

She mulled this over as she followed him back down their trail out of the Dream Hollow Mountains. Ansley couldn't help but feel that she was being pushed through her training much faster than she was ready. She wondered who the "*we*" was that Damon mentioned and how often they discussed her training. It would be so much easier if everyone could just be more upfront with her about what was going on. *What were they keeping from her?*

She sighed and resigned herself to thoughts of the only thing that brought her peace lately: A dark-haired boy with bright blue eyes and a big smile. She was eager to rejoin him that night in their adventures. At least it was the one secret she kept to herself.

THIRTEEN

Kenna

Kenna closed her eyes after she laid her head on her pillow. She felt that familiar tug and let it pull her into a dream.

***

Opening her eyes, she looked around at what appeared to be a small park by a slow-moving river. Kenna did not see anyone under the tall maples that dotted the horizon. It seemed as though the sun would set soon. Colors played over the water like spilled paint, and fallen leaves moved lazily along in the current. It was a pleasant scene. Kenna was thankful for the soothing sunset after a long day of work.

She walked towards a black, stone bench and sat near the water. She could not see her tribe members, but she knew they were nearby. They shared a tether. *It constantly pulled her into dreams that they were working in. That was the tug that had brought her into this one. Lately, her tribe had spent their time working with people who were suffering from losing their loved ones in these mysterious attacks. Dreamwalkers did not often seek to provide comfort, but Jameson and Kenna had requested it. The attacks on Willow were already leaving deep wounds for its people. Kenna hoped that their tribe could distract these victims at night from the horrors they suffered in the day. Jameson was a key part of this process, so he had initiated the dream and pulled the others in with him. He would be the one taking the lead tonight.*

Kenna felt a light breeze tugging her hair over her shoulder. She turned in that direction to see Jameson strolling over a small wooden bridge. He walked alongside an older man who was inspecting the red and yellow tulips growing near the water's edge. She immediately recognized him.

The old man worked on the dock and owned a small fish store, very similar to hers. He was kind, as his features indicated, and he always shared smiles with Kenna at the market. She couldn't quite recall his name. She was shocked to think that he had fallen victim to these attacks too. He was such a kind man. Was he a dreamwalker too?

Kenna puzzled over her thoughts but eventually put them out of her mind and tried to enjoy the pleasant scenery. She often found herself surprised or confused with her tribe's purpose when dreamwalking, but that was the way her tribe worked. They moved together at night, and each member would serve their purpose once in the dream. They didn't always have the answers. Then again, they didn't always need the answers. The tribe was a team and had been for nearly ten years.

Kenna reminisced as she watched Jameson stopping and pointing in the direction of a small flock of ducks that had set out for an afternoon dip in the cool water. When she had determined she was a wielder, she had immediately been encouraged to join a tribe by several dreamwalkers in Willow. Jameson, the leader of her tribe, had been the first to offer her a spot on his team.

As a middle-aged bachelor, Jameson spent most of his spare time in search of new missions for their tribe to complete. He could influence or motivate dreamers to take on any activity or idea that he suggested. He had the skill of persuasion. *It was an odd type of skill, and Kenna wasn't sure how easily Jameson could dedicate himself to using it honorably; however, he was always above the life of a criminal and found himself standing on the moral high ground. She smiled and turned away from her leader, who was now whispering into the old man's ear, to look at the now approaching elderly lady on her right.*

That must be Sophie, *she thought with a laugh. Sophie was around Kenna's age and had joined the tribe not long after she had. Sophie, unlike Kenna, had been branded a shifter. She took advantage of this each night and attempted to disguise herself from everyone, even her tribe members. She was what many called "carefree" and saw dreamwalking as a game to play. She always tried to bring an element of fun into their* walking, but Kenna had to admit that she wished Sophie wasn't so flippant with her responsibilities. It was difficult to get her to understand the gravity of most situations.

Sophie sat beside Kenna and rotated her walking stick to her other wrinkled hand. "Nice evening, don't you think?" She asked as she winked at Kenna.

"What are we doing here?" Kenna asked glancing around the beautiful scene she was emerged in.

"I'm not sure," Sophie said as she pushed her spectacles back up her nose, "but Jameson seems to be at ease. It must be more of an emotional task that he has chosen for us tonight. Have you seen the others?"

"Not yet, but I think we can expect them any time now." Kenna closed her eyes and pulled on that tether herself, urging the others to join them. She felt some acceptance from one direction and silence from the other. "Dane should be joining us soon," she added, wondering silently what kept Laurel. Dane appeared over the top of the hill, and he smiled as he approached the two women on the bench.

"Good evening," he said, nodding at the two women. Dane was a tall man with broad shoulders. He had light brown eyes and curly hair. His skin was dark and gleamed a beautiful shade of ebony when the light fell on him. He smiled, and Kenna noted his straight, pearly white teeth. He was what some would call handsome, and others striking. Unlike most, Kenna had never been impressed. Dane carried himself with an arrogance that made her sick to her stomach. She had never spoken with her other tribe members about it, especially since she knew Sophie had an interest in him.

Dane had joined them only last year and was a wielder like herself. He was always unprepared, if Kenna had to admit it, and his contributions to their tribe's missions were never up to her own standards. Kenna wished he had not joined, but it was not her decision. Dane did have the benefit of being gifted with the element of water. This gift made him a wielder that was eagerly sought after upon his inheritance and training.

Wielders were different than shifters, seers, and persuaders because they could have different skills within their own group. Earth, air, and water were the key elements. Very few were gifted with water, and even less had the element of air, which allowed them to manipulate themselves by flying and creating fire. Kenna was gifted with earth, but that was the gift most wielders had. It made her ordinary, and Dane's gift made him more essential to missions, even if his character did not.

"Why so glum?" Dane asked, not appearing to actually care for an answer. He glanced towards Jameson and the old man on the other side of the park. "Has he said what his scheme is tonight?"

"No, but I assume it's his typical one. Sparing those from loneliness and heartache...." Kenna said as she sighed deeply. *"I'm glad we have been allowed to offer peace to these victims, but why can't we offer more than that? Like an attack plan instead of an after-thought, especially with the recent attacks?"*

"I heard another family was targeted. They were dreamwalkers like the others." Sophie glanced at Dane for his thoughts.

"Yea, who knows? They probably had it coming if we're being honest. They shouldn't have flaunted their skills the way I heard they were doing. I know they had young ones, but talking about them in the square in raised voices? It's asking for it..." Dane picked up a rock from the path and tried to skip it on the water.

"Well, that's not the point is it? The point is that they were killed, and we still don't know why or even how!" Kenna frowned in Dane's direction. He really was a child. *She bit down her disgust..*

"I heard that some groups are investigating near the mountains. They expect-" Sophie was cut off as Jameson approached at a run.

"What are you all doing? Do you have any sense? Stop talking and look around!" His face was red from his sprint and sweat gathered at his graying temples.

Kenna noticed that the scene had changed to a blood red sky. The sun had disappeared, and the coloring wasn't right. "Jameson, what is going on?" She asked softly.

"Someone is coming, and from appearances, it isn't anyone we want to wait around for," Jameson whispered. "We need to get out of here."

Kenna stood hesitantly, just as she saw a group of people enter into their park dream as if they had appeared from thin air. A woman and three men, from what she could make out at this distance. Her heart seemed to stop in her chest as she watched them taking in the newly changed scene. They turned around in a circle. Upon seeing her tribe, they pointed in their direction. The men took off at a run to reach them before Kenna and her friends could escape.

Sophie had shifted into a fish moments before and blended into the dark river that now reflected the blood-red sky. Jameson, unable to defend himself, turned to Dane in desperation.

"Get out of here, Sophie!" Dane exclaimed. He raised his hands slowly above his head, taking great effort to pull as much of the water from the river without displacing his friend who was swimming in the opposite direction. Jameson moved behind Kenna, who he nodded to as well. She knew the routine and was ready. Kenna watched as Dane moved the water into a wall between them and the three men, who were attempting to cross the bridge. They didn't use any skills, *so Kenna thought maybe they had a good chance at making it out of the dream safely.*

She lifted her own hands together in front of her face before pulling them quickly in opposite directions. Just as quickly, the ground gave way under each side of the small bridge. The men fell feet first into the fast-moving water below. Dane took his chance and moved the wall of water on top of the men like a huge tidal wave. Then, Kenna and Jameson ran.

Kenna knew that waking was always a challenge for her, especially when she was under duress. She turned her head briefly to see Jameson disappear into the darkness, and she knew he had made it to safety. Dane continued running beside her until he disappeared as well. She was willing to bet that Sophie was out too but did not pause to look into the water running just as fast beside her. Kenna tried to calm her thoughts so that she could return to her bedroom and her own dreams, but her heart pounded so loudly it made it impossible. She continued to run, glancing over her shoulder frequently for her pursuers, but she never saw them.

Then Kenna hit something. She closed her eyes and tried to shake the stars from her vision. When she opened them, a woman was standing in front of her. She reached out for Kenna and wrapped her hands around Kenna's forearm. The woman was trying to restrain her until the men caught up. Kenna remembered her training. She closed her eyes and took several deep breaths, giving up on attempting to free her arm.

***

When she opened her eyes, Kenna was once again laying in her bed. Edric was snoring softly beside her. Her heart continued to run its race with no ending in sight.

She had escaped, and now their enemy had a face. Kenna couldn't help but feel that this problem was far from being solved. *How had they found them, and what were they trying to do to her? Why hadn't Laurel responded and joined them?* Her thoughts echoed endlessly as she tried to catch her breath in the quiet room. She lay beside Edric and was thankful she had made it home.

FOURTEEN
Ansley

Ansley shook her head in amazement as she surveyed the view below. She sat on the top of a cliff and looked down at the small river that glittered with the first of the morning light. She was thankful to have another night of rest and escape from her dreamvisions. They had been plaguing her since her inheritance ceremony. She couldn't even begin to deal with what had happened in her barn the other night. Ansley swung her legs happily and let herself inhale the fresh air around her- or what she dreamed was fresh air.

She had never understood why dreaming felt almost the same as living, but she guessed it was the same for all dreamwalkers. A piece of her did only exist here anyway, she thought, lifting her fingers to the mark on her forehead. It had been only a week since her inheritance ceremony, roughly a week and a half from her family's funeral, and her life had changed so drastically.

Her family now only existed in her memories, and her existence was badgered by either dreamvisions or her new and grumpy tutor. At least he was settling down some. Since he had arrived, Ansley had noticed a change in Damon. It was in more than just in his appearance.

The man seemed to find some sort of calm here. He was one of them, after all. Ansley couldn't begin to fathom what it would be like to be exiled from your own people. She wondered where he had gone and what he had spent his time doing since then. He seemed to have demons in his past that would not let go of him. At some moments, his kindness would bleed through the huge wall he had put up around himself. In the next breath, he would berate her about something, as if trying to erase the possibility from her mind that he was anything but a brute. What kind of person spent their time trying to convince themselves they were such a monster? *she wondered, almost pitying him.*

Ansley sighed and pushed thoughts of Damon aside. Even in her own dreams, she couldn't escape him. She rolled her eyes. She picked up a small rock lying beside her and dropped it into the ravine. Ansley watched its almost endless descent and wondered what it would be like to fly. She had never even met a wielder who had been gifted the element of air.

Ansley jumped as she heard a sound behind her on the trail. She turned to look and tried to dismiss the fear that was growing in her gut. Maybe it's Nana... *she thought hopefully, but that thought died swiftly as she spotted a stranger.*

"Wondering what it would be like to fall like your rock, little girl?" The woman purred at her. The woman was dressed in all black and had her dingy

129

blonde hair pulled back in a high ponytail. She smiled, but Ansley saw hunger in her eyes.

Ansley rose to her feet and made to move away from the ledge, but the woman blocked her path.

"What do you want?" Ansley asked, steadying her voice.

The woman smiled at her. "What everyone wants, dear," she replied as two others rushed at Ansley. They had been hiding in the brush alongside the ledge. The two men grabbed Ansley by the arms, gripping so hard it hurt. Ansley tried to twist away but was unsuccessful.

She hastened a look at the man who stood a foot taller than her on her right. He had dirt smeared on his hands and face, she presumed to help him blend into his surroundings. His smile was broken by several missing teeth. Ansley turned back to face the woman standing in front of her. The woman tutted at her, in a motherly way. "You should know better not to dream alone. But I guess I should thank you for it. We have been low on supplies lately."

The woman reached out and touched Ansley's face. Ansley tried to shake her off, but the man to her left grabbed her head and held her tightly in place. Suddenly, Ansley felt a wave of calm and peace wash over her. She stopped fighting the men and looked at the woman and waited. The woman smiled again, that hunger flashing in her eyes once more. "You're going to give me your skill. You'll offer it freely."

The words rang through Ansley's mind, and she repeated them softly. "I'm going to give you my skill, and I'll offer it freely." The woman nodded in agreement and reached for a knife that was tucked into her waistband. She cut both their hands. She grabbed Ansley's and held it ready to touch to her own. Ansley watched the scene unfolding, her mind blank and wondered stupidly what would happen next.

Ansley was thrown onto the rocks. The missing teeth man had disappeared. From the screaming she heard, she could only guess where he had gone. A figure stood over Ansley now and advanced towards the other man. It was a man, and he had....he had a sword. Ansley thought. Her thoughts were still muddled, but they had begun to clear. She watched as the man lunged towards her attacker. The attacker dodged him, and the woman attacked Ansley's savior from behind, wrapping her arms around his neck.

Ansley stood quickly and looked around in search of something to help. She had nothing! But then, she spotted a large loose rock. She wrapped both hands around it and lifted it. The pair still struggled in front of her. The woman's accomplice had just drawn a knife from his belt. Ansley ran up behind him and bashed the rock into his skull. He dropped instantly, and Ansley lost her hold on the rock. Ansley eyed her savior after she was certain the man was unconscious. Ansley frowned in recognition of the man. "Rhys?"

"Stay down, *Ansley!" He bellowed at her, those blue eyes full of fear. Rhys lunged at the woman in front of him. She ducked and swept the legs out from under him in a swift movement. As he tried to rise, the woman shook her head and simply said, "Forget it." Then, she disappeared. Rhys and Ansley stared at where she had disappeared in astonishment for a few moments before moving again. Ansley finally found her feet and hurried over to Rhys. She offered him a hand, and he took it, pulling himself back up.*

He looked over her in concern. "Are you okay?" he asked while he tried to determine if Ansley was bleeding or had any injuries.

Ansley ignored his question and said in disbelief, "You're not real."

Rhys stared at her and raised his eyebrows at her statement. "Wow, she really got to you, didn't she? That persuader?"

"What?" Ansley asked, confused. "Well, yes, but no. No! I meant that you are just an element of my dreams. How are you here if you aren't real? Did I bring you here to save me?"

"What do you mean I'm not real? I met you a few nights ago, Ansley! Are you sure you are alright?" A wrinkle appeared across Rhys's forehead, and he reached towards Ansley's shoulder.

Ansley looked at him more closely. She took a step closer and touched his face. His eyes widened, but then those same blue eyes softened. Ansley shook her head and said, "I thought you were someone I had just dreamed on my own. But you're really here?"

"Yes," Rhys said before laughing. He reached up and grabbed Ansley's hand. "I try to check in on you when I can. I saw that they had tracked you here, and I got worried. Sometimes I wish I had a more useful skill, but I did have a dreamvision of this last week. Who knew it was supposed to happen tonight, though?" He added with a smile. "I guess I had good timing."

"Wait. Why are you checking in on me? And who are you really?" Ansley asked, dropping Rhys's hand and backing away from him.

"Ansley, it's alright. I'm not here to hurt you." He said, raising his hands. "Remember when we spoke the other night? I told you I had seen our futures?"

Ansley nodded silently, but she still maintained her distance from him.

"We are linked, you and me. We have been for a long time. That's how I can find you. How I've always been able to find you. I had dreamvisions of you even before I inherited. Since I was a boy."

Ansley's eyes widened and she lowered herself to sit down. To process. Linked? *"But…how?* Why?*"*

Rhys sighed and came to sit next to her. He looked out towards the ravine and took in the view from the cliff, as she had been doing before she had been attacked. "I don't know. But I think we must share a destiny."

Ansley let that sink in. She brushed the strands of hair out of her eyes and looked more closely at Rhys. He was very tall, and he carried himself with confidence. He also seemed to exude an air of loyalty and kindness. He sat quietly, leaving her alone with her thoughts.

"I've never seen you before." Ansley stated. Rhys turned away from the view to look back at Ansley.

"I know." He said simply, knowing she wasn't meaning the other night. "I didn't think you were ready."

"So, what made you think I was ready now?" She asked stubbornly.

Rhys turned back to the view, and the sun shone brightly on his face. The light made his eyes sparkle like the river below them. "I didn't think that you were. I just knew you needed me."

Ansley looked back out at the calm scene bathed in morning light. She mulled over those words and knew she couldn't deny them. She did need somebody right now. *She just wondered if he was the right one to fill that empty space.*

FIFTEEN

Kenna
One day after the attack

Kenna sat across from Laurel in her small flat. She had never been here before. She had never met any of her tribe members in person before. The uniqueness of the situation struck her as she looked around at Jameson, Dane, Sophie, and Edric. She had never imagined that events would bring her tribe and husband together, but the circumstances had changed.

Edric was a *typical*, but he had been let in on Kenna's secret early into their relationship. After about six months of seeing each other, Kenna had unexpectedly traveled into Edric's dreams. It had been an accident, but what happened in the dream definitely wasn't. Kenna remembered seeing Edric the very next day and how her cheeks had burned with heat. She had decided if they were to be in a healthy relationship, he should know the whole story. Edric's easy-going nature had prevailed. He had smiled seductively and simply said, "Well, I'll be expecting to see you every night then."

Kenna looked back at her other companions, trying to shake the memory away. Laurel sat on her large, cozy couch in a black silk kimono, arms crossed with a disturbed look on her face. Her red hair was trimmed short, above her ears, and her face was smattered with freckles across the bridge of her nose and cheeks. Her brilliant green eyes were striking, and they seemed to cut into Kenna.

Laurel had not responded to the "call" to join her tribe because she had been *detained,* as Dane had referred to it earlier. When they had escaped the old-man's-dream-turned-nightmare, her tribe had entered Jameson's own dream and discussed what had happened. They were all very concerned about the attack, but even more so about Laurel. Ever since she had become a member of their tribe four years earlier, she *always* responded. She was not the friendliest of the group, but she was very dependable.

Jameson had known immediately that something was wrong. He had insisted on a meeting the next day. Because they sensed his distress, the others had agreed. The tribe had met at a small restaurant on a dock that was about fifteen miles outside of Wusylla, to the south of Willow. Jameson had explained that meeting here would draw less attention because others may assume they were travelers. They had all arrived separately and again were disturbed that Laurel was not present.

They had immediately departed the pier for Laurel's small flat. Jameson was the only member who had access to their addresses in case of emergency. Concerned about their safety, Kenna had sent a messenger for Edric, and nobody except Dane had seemed to mind.

"Why should we trust a typical to protect our secrets? He may be *your husband*, but he is nothing to us," Dane had complained.

"You may be a big shot elsewhere, but *here* you are no better than Edric. And you might prefer him to be there, so *you* don't get your ass kicked," Kenna had said angrily before walking briskly after Sophie and Jameson. Dane had not responded, but there they were. Edric stood beside her at the table without anyone objecting.

Upon arriving to Laurel's flat, they had found the door askew. Dane and Edric had taken the lead and crossed quietly through the entrance. Edric had his bow drawn, and Dane carried a short sword. Nobody had greeted them, so they had continued their search of the small flat. Kenna had noticed Laurel's meager belongings scattered and broken on the floor. Their group had stalked around the flat before finally finding Laurel on her stomach under the bed. She was unconscious, and her hands and feet had been tied. It looked like she had crawled under the bed to hide before passing out. Blood matted her hair over her left temple and had dripped down her face. There was a small red stain on the rug below her chin.

Jameson gently pulled her out from under the bed, and Kenna tended to her injury. After being roused with cool water on her face, Laurel had almost drop-kicked Dane, who had been standing over her. Jameson gently reached for Laurel's shoulder. She flinched but calmed down quickly. "Why are you here?" She had whispered in a frightened tone.

Kenna and Jameson took turns explaining what had happened the night before, and then it was Laurel's turn. "I was attacked here early in the night. I was just finishing dinner, and someone came in from one of the back windows. I never saw his face. He knocked me out cold before I could turn around, and when I woke, he had bound my hands and feet." Laurel had trembled while she explained what had happened. Sophie reached out her hand and placed it on Laurel's shoulder.

"We are so glad that you are all right," she said with a soft smile. Kenna turned to look at her tribe member. *Really* look at her for the first time. It struck Kenna that this was the only time she had seen what Sophie really looked like. Kenna smiled as she took in Sophie's amber eyes and beautiful light brown skin. She was curvy for her height, and formidable.

"But *are* you?" Jameson asked, drawing Kenna's attention back to Laurel. "Why was he here?"

"He wanted my skill," Laurel whispered. She looked up into Jameson's face with terror as she added, "He tried to lure me into a dream, but I held him off, so he couldn't do anything else except kill me. It was obvious that wasn't his only intention, so he walked back to the window and climbed out. He told me he would be back with others."

"Wait, he left you here?" Edric asked, frowning with confusion.

"Yes. I crawled under the bed to hide when he left. After I made it under the bed, I guess I passed out from the pain. He kicked me hard in the ribs when he was binding my hands," Laurel said, touching her ribs gingerly. "I tried to fight back."

Kenna glanced at Edric, who was now checking all the entryways to the flat. "It isn't safe here. Not for any of you. We must leave as soon as we can." He turned and looked desperately at Kenna who got his message loud and clear: *They will be here soon.*

"Can you walk?" Jameson asked Laurel.

"I don't think so. My right leg gave out when I tried to stand. I think it may be broken from my fall earlier."

"Then Dane will carry you," Jameson said, looking back at Dane to silently give the order.

"There was something else," Laurel said softly. Jameson and Sophie both looked back at Laurel, and Kenna noticed their concern. "I heard him mention something...a stone...or something like that. It seemed important to him."

Jameson leaned back against the couch cushions and nodded silently. He frowned but didn't tell the others what he was thinking. "Alright. We need to get you somewhere safe. Dane?"

Dane rolled his eyes before stepping up to Laurel, who wrapped her arms around his neck. He lifted her from her chair, and a small whimper escaped her lips as Dane turned swiftly and hurried to the door. They each waited five minutes before departing after Dane, to make it appear that they were not together.

Kenna's heart began pounding as she and Edric left, the last of the group to depart. Edric looped his arm through hers and took an easy pace. He laughed once, trying to make it seem like they were a carefree couple out for a morning stroll. Kenna couldn't help but sense that eyes were following them as she turned the corner to walk back to their meeting place on the pier.

***

Kenna and Edric had insisted on the group joining them for lunch at their flat. Everyone was exhausted from the events of the morning, and they needed a place to hide out while they formulated a plan.

Kenna had helped Laurel change into a spare set of her clothes, and Laurel was now resting on the guest bed. Kenna closed the door to the bedroom quietly before rejoining her tribe in the kitchen. Edric had just started heating water for more coffee.

"She finally fell asleep. I think the tea and the tonic helped her relax," Kenna said as she slid into a chair at the table.

"Let's hope we have enough stored to last her through the week. She is going to need it," Edric said matter-of-factly.

"Jameson, you can't overlook it any longer," Kenna exclaimed, "We have been thrust into some sort of war. We may not know our enemy, but they know us! They are acting quickly now, and so should we."

Jameson stirred his coffee and frowned. He looked around at Sophie, eating her stew, and Dane, who was leaning against the windowsill and checking the street for anyone suspicious that might have followed them here. "Are we sure that this wasn't just a local? People are attacked all the time. Just because Laurel is a dreamwalker, doesn't mean that she was targeted."

Just like Jameson to avoid the facts. The man would deny danger even if someone was threatening him with a drawn weapon. Kenna glanced at Edric, who shook his head slightly. *Don't go there, Kenna*, she seemed to read from his face. She sighed, but he was right. She wasn't in the mood to argue after her friend had been attacked.

"Regardless, she was attacked, and we know that someone is targeting dreamwalkers. I think it's time to take action."

"What do you propose?" Sophie asked cautiously, never eager to volunteer.

"I propose going to the elders of Terra. They are the chief elders of Arvenia, and their historian is rumored to have a library of ancient scrolls and manuscripts of dreamwalkers from the last several centuries. If anyone is likely to know what is happening, it would be them," Kenna said.

"*If* something is going on," Jameson corrected her, still looking down at his coffee cup.

Kenna felt her fire grow and waited for steam to shoot out of her ears. She chewed on the inside of her cheek as her temper puttered out. Dane turned to face his companions.

"I volunteer." He said simply.

"*What*?" Kenna asked, bewildered.

"*Why*?" Sophie asked softly. Kenna shot a dirty look her way, and Sophie quickly returned it to her. "Well, it's not like it would be easy or safe."

"I've always wanted to see Avendale," Dane said before turning back to the window. His eyes showed determination, but he seemed aloof.

Kenna snorted, but she didn't want to press her luck. "Well, I suppose it is a good opportunity to travel. Of course, *I* will go too. This was my idea, and I want to find answers. Edric?" She asked.

"I would very much like to go with you, but Kenna, someone needs to look out for your tribe. I may be *typical,* but I am smart. I would like to keep an eye on things here while you are gone."

Kenna's heart seemed to rip in half, but he was right. Taking him with her would be selfish when he was needed here. Jameson was an older man, and Sophie and Laurel could not protect themselves in daylight. They needed muscle. Edric would see to it that they were safe. By doing so, he was protecting her interests too. Besides, he *was* a typical. If these people were after dreamwalkers, he wouldn't be in danger.

Kenna sighed. "Well, what do you think, Jameson?"

Jameson reached out his hand to shake Edric's. "I'm honored that a typical would offer to help us," he said while thanking Edric. "I can't say I agree that you need to go, Kenna, but if you must, I won't stop you." He came over to stand beside her. "It looks like we have a solid plan." Kenna wrapped her arms around Jameson's neck and hugged him tightly. He was the closest thing to a father she had had in many years. Even though he was difficult sometimes, he had always listened to her. She planted a small kiss on his cheek before releasing him.

"Yeah, I guess we do."

SIXTEEN
Rosalie

Rosalie hurried into the Dream Hollow Mountains with a small bag of supplies on her shoulder. She walked so quickly that she could hardly see her feet under her as they snagged on the undergrowth. Roots seemed to lift from the ground to grab her as she traveled far from her once happy home. Her vision was clouded with the image of her dead husband on the floor, staring up at her from his newly cold brown eyes. She couldn't shake the horror she had felt when she found him. His handsome face had seemed shriveled with wrinkles, and his blonde hair had turned white.

Rosalie sobbed as she quickened her steps into a run. She ran as fast as the brush would allow, and her pack jostled angrily on her back, thumping her with every step. It felt like it was beating the life out of her, or maybe the memory of Stephen was doing that. She choked on the thought of his name and found herself flung to the ground. *Damn root!* She thought angrily.

Rosalie sat and rested as she recalled the last hour. She had hastily grabbed an empty potato sack and filled it to the brim with extra clothes, candles to light her way in the dark, food, and Stephen's ax. *How she wished he had that in hand earlier!* Rosalie covered her face with her hands and tried to pull herself together. After gathering her necessities, she had fled to the mountains without bothering to warn the neighbors. She knew what this was, and there was no use in trying to save them. *They were already gone.*

The darkness had spread throughout the sky in a matter of minutes after Stephen's attack. The sun, her best ally, had been taken from her, and she knew that with this darkness came death. Trouble lurked in its shadows, and trouble would try its best to find her.

Years ago, she had started having the dreamvisions of this night. She knew this would come to pass, and it finally had. Her way of life was gone now. The only choice she had was to live. She laid her hand gently over her belly.

"I know you don't know me yet, young one, but I *will* protect you. We *will* survive this, you and me. One day, all it will be is a bad memory." Rosalie wiped her other hand across her face to erase proof of her tears once more, before finally rising to her feet again.

She shouldered her potato sack and resumed a slower pace. She caught her breath and turned her face to the highest peak of the mountain as she trudged onward. To safety, her new home, and away from death. The darkness concealed her destination, but she knew the steps from walking them regularly when she was a child. Her feet would take her back home to the mountain.

SEVENTEEN

Kenna

Kenna lifted a spoon of beef stew to her mouth but paused as she sensed his stare. She turned to her left and looked at Dane. His eyes gleamed like embers. "Yes?" Kenna asked, her annoyance clear in her tone.

Dane dropped his gaze, reaching for his own spoon. "Nothing. Nothing." He replied, taking a large bite of potato.

Kenna rolled her eyes and returned to her stew. They had been traveling for two days now, and Dane was really starting to get under her skin. They ate the rest of their meal at the small inn in silence, and Kenna was thankful for it. She was tired. She couldn't remember the last time she had ridden for two days straight. Her thighs and hips were starting to protest, and every step seemed a chore. But, they had made it to the outer edge of the Forest of Visions. They need only continue through the woods to reach Terra. Unfortunately, there had always been a mystery about these woods. Men had entered and lost their way, not to be heard from again. She shifted her weight on the wooden bench, trying to find a comfortable position as she tried to focus on something pleasant.

Dane laughed at her over his cup of ale, prompting a dark look from Kenna. She stood from the bench and walked toward the woman drying cups near the bar. A man sat in front of her, and they talked loudly, laughing and smiling like old friends. When Kenna approached, the woman turned away from her friend and said, "What can I get you, dear?"

"Just another cup of ale, if you don't mind." Kenna handed her empty cup to the woman. The woman smiled at her and nodded. She turned away to fill Kenna's cup, and the man at the bar looked over at Kenna. He nodded at her stance and said, "Looks like you've had a day or two in the saddle."

Kenna nodded. "I am from Willow. We are passing through on our way to Terra."

The man took a swig from his own cup of ale. "Honeymoon?" He asked, not really interested in her answer.

Kenna's eyebrows rose, and she turned to look at Dane, who sat smirking at her. He had heard the question too. Kenna cleared her throat, and replied, "No. We are…family."

"Hmm." The man replied, eyeing Kenna. The woman returned with her cup of ale, and Kenna hastened back to her table. Dane laughed as she approached. "Looks like I'm not the only one who thinks you are easy on the eyes, Fischer."

"Don't start," Kenna replied. "Don't you have some young, naïve girl to chase after? Instead of bothering with a married woman?"

"I always thought the challenging ones were the most fun." Dane said, smiling into his cup of ale.

Kenna rolled her eyes at him again. "Why do you have to be such a prick?"

"Your face turns this lovely shade of red when you are angry, and I like the way you glare at me. We've got a long road ahead of us. Don't rob me of my simple pleasures," Dane replied.

Kenna shook her head. *How had she gotten stuck with such a tasteless travel companion?* She tried to change the subject and deflect her own anger and annoyance with him. "You know you've never spoken much about your family. What are they like?"

Dane shrugged. "Nothing special. Well, my father thinks he is, but he is even more of a prick than I am, believe me or not."

Kenna frowned, trying to understand Dane. He continued, "My mother is the best of us. She keeps me sane. I don't know how she puts up with any of us, my father especially. He doesn't deserve her."

Kenna tried to hide the surprise on her face. *Dane? Talking about a woman without being a jerk? This was definitely a first.*

He saw the look on her face and guessed at her thoughts. "What? Never pegged me as a momma's boy?" Dane chuckled. The sound echoed deep in his throat. "You may think you know everything, but you don't know a damn thing about me, Kenna." He took another sip of ale. "What about you? With a face like yours I'd think you had everything come easy to you," he added. Resentment edged his words.

Kenna took a deep breath. "Not quite."

Dane looked at her closely. "What were your trials like? Mine were *horrible*, but my father agreed that I'd lucked out with my skill. You know, I don't think I've ever heard you talk about your trials."

"Because I haven't," Kenna said as she stood from the table, ale in her hand. "I'm going to sleep, Dane. I suggest you get some rest yourself."

He looked at her, suspicion lining his handsome face. Then he shrugged, "Suit yourself."

Kenna left him at the table and walked toward the small flight of steps leading up to the room they had rented. Unfortunately, they would have to share. They didn't have much gold in their travel bags, and they had both agreed to hold onto as much as they could. She opened the worn wooden door and walked inside. She went to one of the small cots and pulled her boots off. Her thighs protested as she leaned over to pick up her discarded travel bag. She dug inside as she remembered Edric's send-off.

He had held her tightly and kissed her deeply that morning before she left their flat. "I know you won't listen to me, but be careful, Kenna. Don't get yourself into something you can't come back from."

He had stroked her hair and kissed her once more. "I *need* you to come back from this in one piece."

She had merely nodded and kissed him back before picking up her travel bag and leaving him standing in their doorway. She had been glad that her tears hadn't started until she made it to the barn two blocks away from their building. She had wiped the tears angrily away before approaching the man at the gate and offering him gold to rent one of his horses. She had hoped that wouldn't be the last time she saw her husband.

As she crawled into her bed, her thoughts centered on Edric, wondering if it had been a mistake to take on this mission. She closed her eyes and prayed to the gods for their guidance before falling quickly into a dreamless sleep.

EIGHTEEN
Ansley

Ansley sat on a stone wall at the edge of a stream with her feet dangling in the cool water. It was refreshing and gave her relief from the steamy heat of the sun. She sat in anticipation, wondering when Rhys would arrive. Their dreams had been fun and relaxing, a happy escape from her training.

This was the fourth night in a row that she had traveled by herself and simply waited for him. *He was reliable and joined her when he had entered the dream realm. Rhys always approached her with that same calm and happy nature. A smile playing across his handsome features and a twinkle in his blue eyes that Ansley liked to think was only for her.*

She drew circles in the water with her big toe, thinking of the adventures they had shared the last few nights. Some were extravagant. Others were simply peaceful and gave the two time to talk to each other, sharing ideas and dreams for their lives. Rhys was a bit older than her, and Ansley enjoyed listening to him speak of his time since his inheritance ceremony. He shared freely, knowing that she too had been through the horrors of the trials.

Her favorite topic was his childhood. He spoke of mountains and living in the wild lands south of

Avendale, to the east of the Balsom River, with his mother and father. He had mentioned a brother, but it seemed to be a touchy subject. Ansley accepted that he wasn't ready to delve into why, so she eagerly steered him to happier conversations when this one was broached.

Her mind reeled with the joy she had experienced just being in his presence. She couldn't believe there was another seer she could talk to besides Damon. They both talked about their triggers, and she was surprised to know that his trigger was a smell. Rhys said that instead of sage, he crushed lavender to trigger a dreamvision. Ansley was secretly jealous of the ease at which he could bring on his visions. She put those thoughts aside as she focused on the hope that had started to grow within her. If Rhys could survive training and use his skill to be helpful to his family and tribe, she knew that maybe she could too.

Ansley had eventually brought up the attacks in Terra. Rhys did not seem taken aback by the gruesome details of the murders. Instead, he shared that some of his friends had also been taken in the same way one night. They bonded over their fears of these attackers, and Ansley tried to understand the comfort she found in this boy sitting before her.

She smiled as she thought of the curves of his face and felt her face grow hot, thinking of how his lips must taste. They had not kissed yet. Though Ansley eagerly looked forward to that moment, she hesitated. She had never kissed anyone before, and she feared the worst when Rhys realized how inexperienced she was. She tried to mask her insecurities, but she found this was not needed. Rhys did not seem overeager to move their relationship to this point. So, Ansley waited. Maybe tonight? She thought anxiously as she contin- ued to move her feet in the cool water below. A water- fall tumbled over rocks several feet ahead and became a shallow stream as it wound away from the falls. The steady roar from the waterfall masked all other sounds to Ansley's ears, and she was surprised when someone gently touched her shoulder.

Ansley started and fell from her seat on the wall into the stream. The water that had been refreshing on her feet was now unbearably freezing. She sat up in the stream, which was only two feet deep, and tried to push her dripping hair from her face. A delightful sound filled her ears from behind the stone wall. She turned to find Rhys bent over in laughter. The water, now drip- ping from her nose and chin, seemed a strong contrast to the temperature of her face.

Ansley stood slowly from the stream and said playfully, "Most men would be polite and help the girl out of the water instead of just laughing at her."

Rhys was unable to stifle his laughter enough to reply. He moved quickly forward and held out his hand to help Ansley step over the wall between them.

He gulped down a deep breath of air before saying, "Ansley, I'm so sorry....I-I didn't mean to-"

Ansley took his hand and instead of pulling herself with it, she tugged on Rhys's arm, throwing him off balance and over the short stone wall. He tumbled hands-first into the stream beside Ansley. When he pushed himself up into a sitting position, Ansley giggled, expecting him to be furious. He turned towards her and let out a booming laugh. He cupped his hand in the water and sent a giant wave in her direction. Ansley, unprepared, got a mouthful. She retaliated by returning a wave. They laughed and played in the stream until the cold wind sent them in search of warmth.

Rhys had offered her a hand in climbing the wall. Then, he swiftly climbed up behind Ansley and walked over to join her, where she had reclaimed her original seat on the stone wall. She shivered as the breeze moved through the weeds surrounding the stream. Rhys sat beside her and put an arm over her shoulders to help warm her.

"If only I was a wielder, I could impress you with a roaring fire," he said. Ansley smiled and looked up at Rhys who sat nearly a head taller than herself. She laid her head on his shoulder before replying, "Yea, I guess you'll have to impress me some other way."

Rhys grew quiet, but after some time, he kissed Ansley's forehead. "Suppose we meet in person some time. Do you think we could be more than just...a dream to each other?"

Ansley turned, shocked by his statement. "Of course, we can. Rhys, I...like you very much." Her cheeks grew warm, and she smiled sheepishly.

The sun had started to fall, and the world seemed to explode with pink and orange. Rhys's eyes glinted as he smiled back at Ansley.

"I like you very much too." He then wrapped his arm around her shoulder once more, pulling her into his side. Ansley rested her head comfortably on his shoulder. They sat there for what seemed hours, watching the sun drop below the horizon to be replaced in the sky by a bright, full moon.

NINETEEN
Kenna

After they had left the small inn outside of the Forest of Visions, Kenna and Dane ventured into the famed woods. They had spent days walking in circles and avoiding all the brush. After spending nearly every waking moment with the man, Kenna could barely stand to be in Dane's presence anymore. They had set up camp in the woods for the night to catch up on the rest they so desperately needed.

Dane was trying to make a small fire with twigs he had collected. Even the things he did to help irritated Kenna. She let out a sigh and reached into her pack to see what food they had left. She pulled out a small loaf of bread, some jerky, and a hunk of cheese that had begun to mold. Using her knife, she cut off that part and tossed it into the shadowy brush.

Their past week had been spent amongst typicals in the villages along the way to Terra. Kenna knew that the council there would have answers, but she had no idea how to find them. Dane had suggested that they spend their days traveling within the villages to monitor the typicals for word of attacks. At night, Jameson joined either Dane or herself in a dream to update them on the attacks closest to home. There had only been one more, but the dreamwalker had died as a result. Also, they had found more clues pointing to who was responsible. A small circle with an arrow below it had been drawn on the floor of the dreamwalker's home. Jameson was unsure of the meaning, but now their tribe was also searching for answers in Willow. Dane suggested that their tribe spend time with their local historian to see if there was any record of the symbols. That was probably the last good suggestion he had made.

Dane was an irritating travel companion. He had insisted that they stop each night instead of traveling on like Kenna had originally planned. He also insisted that they infiltrate typicals' dreams each night, but Kenna wasn't entirely sure why. She felt the idea was a good one until they had spent a week looking for answers with not one to be found. Kenna had determined that they would only have success through dreams from other dreamwalkers, which they could not reach unless invited. She had abandoned their charade of "dream-stalking" to allow herself a few hours of rest at night, in hopes that she would feel recharged for the next day. Dane had continued to look for clues in the dreams of those nearby. He was stubborn and had not agreed with her decisions at any turn.

She missed Edric. To her delight, she had finally found him last night. They had a happy reunion until Dane showed up to remind her that she couldn't sleep all morning. He had popped into her dream at an unfortunate time. Even though he didn't mention it on their journey today, she knew he smirked at her when she wasn't looking. No one, literally *no one*, had ever interfered with her dreams with Edric. It was forbidden amongst dreamwalkers to disturb dreams between spouses at any time. This was a bond that was considered sacred among them, and it was not meant to be dishonored. She would have to find a way later to exact her revenge on Dane, but now wasn't the right time. She glanced once again at the mystery that was Dane, finally successful with the small fire he had been trying to light for the last fifteen minutes. *How could such a talented dreamwalker be so useless in the real world?*

"Staring isn't polite, you know," Dane murmured as he moved away from the fire to unroll his bedroll.

"You should take your own advice sometime." Kenna said as she focused her attention on splitting the remaining food into two equal servings.

"Take my cheese. It didn't taste good the last time we ate it, and I don't want to risk it," Dane said before Kenna could hand him his half.

She glared at him before adding the extra piece to her meager portions.

"How far until we reach Terra?" Dane asked, chewing his bread meticulously.

"I think we have one more day of walking left, and there should be a small village on the outskirts of the fields of Terra. We should stop there for the night before moving on."

Dane shrugged as he tossed his bread crust into the fire that had grown enough to warm Kenna's face. "I'm going to sleep. You coming tonight, or do you prefer...*other entertainment?*" He asked with a smile. Kenna glared at him once again, and Dane shrugged in response.

"Suit yourself." He laid down on his bedroll and turned away from her. She watched him leave for the dream realm almost immediately. This was the price of joining a tribe, *an eternal bond*. Kenna had always thought it was more of a sibling bond that anything else. With the way they bickered, who could suggest anything different?

Kenna looked up at the stars. She quickly found the Star of the North and followed it down to the Bear, the largest constellation. To its right, Kenna spotted the River and the Serpent. Beneath both of them, the Hunter. It took her several moments to find her own constellation, the Fish. It was one of the hardest ones to find in the night sky, even on a clear night. All Fischers had been taught how to locate it. Whenever Kenna looked up and saw her family's stars, she thought of her uncle. He had been a kind man, but he hadn't been a part of her life for very long. Kenna had spent maybe two years in his home before a fever had taken him. He was also much older than Kenna's parents would have been if they had been living.

The oldest dreamwalker in his family, her Uncle James had lived in Willow his entire life. He was an elderly bachelor, probably in his late fifties when he took in Kenna. She had been orphaned at age 3 and lucky to find a home with the kind man. She called him "uncle", but in reality, they were not blood relatives. That never stopped her from loving him.

Uncle James was a wielder, like herself, but he had the gift of *air*. He could move air in dreams to make things fly, typically Kenna. She smiled as she remembered him floating her higher than the treetops so that she could get a good glimpse of the sea. She could see the dolphins jumping far off in the distance. She sighed, wondering if he had been able to make fire, as she watched their own fire burning in the dark night. Most wielders who worked with air could, but Uncle James had never shared much of his dreamwalking with Kenna. The man had preferred to dreamwalk alone, and he had never joined a tribe. Her uncle had preferred to remain uninvolved in the dreamwalkers' calling.

Family or not, Uncle James had been kind to her, taking her in when she had no one. She was only six when he found her and eight when he died. Her eyes moistened with love for the man she had barely known. She wondered deep down if he would be proud of the mission she had volunteered for. *A silly thought*, she told herself as she slouched down into her bedroll. The man had never even known that his sweet Kenna possessed a skill.

Kenna laid her head on the ground and closed her eyes. She floated into a deep, deep sleep where she soared far above the trees to touch the sky. Her dreams were pleasant and refreshing. A welcome reprieve from her hard day of travel.

***

Confusion filled Kenna as she felt herself come back from her dream. She had just been soaring past a small flock of seagulls toward the Glass Sea. She frowned at Dane as he tried to communicate with her. Something important, by the look on his face.

"…in the village. They were dead, Kenna. We don't have much time!" Kenna sat up from her bedroll. "What?" She asked shaking the dreaminess away.

"I *said*, there was another attack in the village near us. Someone was attacked, and I heard their screams. *Didn't you hear it?* We have to move fast if we want to catch them." Dane was not frantic but practical, as if planning a weekend vacation. "If the attackers fled into the mountains, we have to move quickly if you want to find them."

"Wait, how do you know they are who we are searching for, and what advantage do we have against them, Dane?" Kenna was surprised to hear herself whisper into that uncertain darkness outside the glow of their now-small fire.

"We are two wielders who know more about what we are facing than the typicals do. *We* have a hell of a better chance than *they* do," Dane replied, ignoring her first question. With that, he shouldered his pack and stomped out the fire with his heavy boot.

Kenna hurriedly gathered her things in the dark. She glanced up once more at the Bear and then to the Fish. She whispered a silent prayer to her ancient elders and her uncle, if he happened to be paying attention. It may be worthless, but she hoped it was worth the effort. She then turned to follow Dane into the darkness that beckoned from deep in the woods.

TWENTY
Ansley

Ansley had only met Rhys in her dream a week before, but her thoughts were consumed with him. She sat cross-legged in the brush of the Dream Hollow Mountains, her back leaned against a tall pine. Her mind drifted to him smiling at her once more. A hint of a smile crossed her own lips as Damon walked back to their small camp for the day of training.

"I filled your canteen," Damon said as he tossed it to her, almost hitting her in the face. He seemed to size her up with those eyes, as black as the bottom of the sea.

"What have you been doing? *Daydreaming?* Don't you take any of this seriously?" He shook the short, wavy locks out of his face and sat down in front of her. "I told you to practice meditating while I was away, and you had an hour to do so. Did you waste time, when time is so precious to *your* people?" Damon scowled with his last comment, taking a sip from his newly refilled flask. He looked toward the sky where the sun had reached its mid-day peak.

Ansley frowned. How would he understand how she felt at all? He was old, and he had probably never felt this way about anyone before. *Worthless old traitor.* She kept her thoughts to herself as she formulated a careful response.

"I was *not* daydreaming. I was thinking about how to pull myself from the dreams like you said. Whether you believe it or not, *Damon,* I am not wasting *your* time." Ansley looked him straight in the eye as she injected as much attitude as possible into her response. "Not that I am ungrateful, but why do you care about helping us anyway?" Ansley asked as she reached for her pack. She pulled out the two bundles of food that her grandmother had packed for them before sunrise. Ansley laid one near Damon's boot, eager to avoid his touch. Damon reached for the offering. Ansley's efforts were not lost on him.

"Being a traitor doesn't mean that you have no feelings, you know." He took a large bite of turkey from the bundle and followed it with several small grapes. "I was only a young one when I betrayed my people. Being exiled changes a man."

Ansley rolled her eyes. "Sure, it does. Well I'm sure you'll make the most of this opportunity to repair the damage you did." She took a bite of cheese and washed it down with water from her canteen. "Why are you still here anyway? Five days have passed, so I thought you would be leaving by now."

Damon said nothing but went rigid. His hand reached out quickly, dropping the piece of meat he had been eating onto the ground. Ansley looked at him in fear as she noticed his eyes rolling back in his head. He reached out to her again with his left hand, "Now Ansley!" he growled through clenched teeth.

Ansley glanced at the sage that she had left burning while Damon was away. She instantly understood and reached her hand out for his. He was holding back his vision so that she could follow him into it. She took his rough, callused hand and the world around her gave way to another one...

***

Ansley stood beside Damon and surveyed where they were. It looked like a small village. Damon brought his finger to his lips to indicate silence and pointed in the direction toward the village. She followed him, trying to keep her footsteps as quiet as possible. Suddenly, a scream echoed out from up ahead. Damon took off at a trot and followed several of the typicals that ran into the small cottage to determine what was amiss.

Damon stopped suddenly, and Ansley barely caught herself before she smashed into him. She couldn't see over his shoulder, so she eased around his frame. Ansley's eyes widened as she beheld a familiar scene. A man and woman lay sprawled on the floor with a small girl laying near them. All of their eyes were wide, staring up as if in surprise. The girl, only around five or six, had a small stab wound to her chest. Ansley's cry died in her throat as she looked closely at the girl. Her golden hair lay fanned around her head, and her amber eyes were open, gazing forever upon whoever had taken her life from her. Ansley looked back at the man and woman to find them both wrinkled with white hair. She silently sank to the ground before Damon remembered she was there. He turned to her and grasped her sharply by the wrist.

***

The vision was replaced quickly by dead leaves laying around her feet, sounds of birds chirping, and sunlight falling through the tall pines above. Ansley drew in a deep breath and closed her eyes. When she opened them, she saw Damon pick up his turkey and take another bite of his lunch.

"Finally, their secrets have led me to them, and it seems like the killers are on the move again."

Despite the vision Damon had just shared with her, they spent the afternoon training. Ansley grew more exhausted as the minutes ticked past. He took her into dreams at least six times after their vision, pushing her as hard as he could. He not only trained her on how to come out of dreams on her own, but he also showed her how to dodge other dreamwalkers and their skills. Being a seer meant that her skill was used to see and learn. This left her vulnerable to all attacks. Damon was a good teacher, but even he didn't seem to notice the young man who appeared in all of Ansley's dreams today. He stayed at a distance and smiled when Ansley looked his way. His blue eyes glittered mischievously with the secret they shared.

***

It was in their final dream together that Damon noticed something was off. "We are not alone here." Damon said glancing around the busy city of Avendale that had materialized around them. "Leave, like I told you to," Damon ordered while trying to sense where the other dreamwalker was.

Ansley laughed and replied defiantly, "Damon, I am not going anywhere. You are just being para-noid." She turned away from Damon in the direction of Rhys and winked.

"Don't disobey me, Ansley!" Damon growled. "When I say we are leaving, we are leaving!" He grasped her wrist again and pulled her out of the dream.

***

"What was that about?" Damon asked angrily upon their return. Ansley sat across from him gasping for air, as she always did when a dream ended.

"*What*?" she asked hesitantly.

"There was someone there, and you knew it. You put us in danger!"

"Give it a rest, Damon." Ansley said gasping out each word.

"We are done for today. Get your things or don't. You can find your own way back to the house.

Don't bother me again until you stop playing your foolish games like a *child*," Damon said, his black eyes burning as he stalked away angrily.

Ansley watched him go. She listened for the crunch of his footsteps to fade. Then, she returned to the dream.

***

She appeared right where they had vanished, on the street near the food vendors. Rhys caught her eye from where he stood near the man selling melons and began walking to her.

Ansley's thoughts seemed muddled. She watched Rhys walk closer and felt as if she were under a spell. She smiled at him and felt the warmth of his smile in return.

"It's good to be able to talk at last," Rhys said as he motioned to a small table away from the vendors. Others were sitting nearby and eating their purchases, admiring the bargains they had made in the square. It still amazed Ansley how real all of this could feel.

"Have you been following me all day?" Ansley asked, her cheeks warming.

"Of course, I have. But not following, more like waiting. Waiting for an opportunity to get to spend more time together." Rhys smiled as he looked at his hands. "I promise I am not trying to stalk you, but I just feel...drawn to you, Ansley."

"It's funny you say that. I feel drawn to you too. Like I've known you for so long," Ansley said softly, barely able to hear her voice over the people walking and talking joyfully around them. She looked down at her own hands, trying to hide the emotion on her face. She was such a silly, little girl! A touch warmed her chin as his hand lifted her face up towards his. Rhys smiled once more as he glanced at her lips. Then, he leaned in and kissed her softly. His lips felt like velvet, and the fire that spread from them was intoxicating.

Ansley froze as she felt heat spread throughout her entire face. She waited until he pulled away, and then suddenly, she felt herself leaving the dream. "No..." she whispered softly to herself as she closed her eyes again.

***

When Ansley opened her eyes once more, she was back in the mountains, and the sun was quickly disappearing from the sky. She smiled and gingerly touched her lips. She couldn't believe that she had left by accident at such a moment. She gave herself one more moment to remember what his lips had felt like against hers before she rose to gather her things. She left the mountains as darkness pushed in around her, but Ansley could only feel the sun shining on her face from the dream she had just awoken from.

TWENTY-ONE

By the time Ansley made the long trek out of the Dream Hollow Mountains to her grandmother's home, all color had long since faded from the sky and left only bright stars twinkling against the darkness. They sparkled as she crossed the field to the front door of the house. It almost seemed as if the stars winked at her, aware of her secret acquaintance and eager to share.

Ansley opened the door and unwound the thick shawl from her shoulders. She reached up to hang it on one of the iron hooks set into the wall as her ears caught the last few words of the conversation in the adjoining room.

"...another family. I can't believe it's happening so quickly. They sent word that they think the perpetrators are fleeing into the mountains. A search team has been assembled and will leave town at any minute. These could be the attackers from the vision you had."

"We have no quarrel with these people."

"*No quarrel?*" Her grandmother's voice broke as it rose in anger. "My son and his family were *slaughtered* by these people. I would think that is reason enough to go after them."

Ansley edged into the kitchen to join the conversation.

"Nana is right. If there is a chance of catching them, I want to try and help too. "Damon met her stare unflinchingly. His dark eyes bore into Ansley's very being, and she found herself looking away first.

"*You*? What would you do to help? You can't even follow the simple rules I give you in training. You would only be a nuisance and likely slow us down."

Ansley's cheeks burned, but she offered no rebuttal. She merely turned to her grandmother and said, "Nana, we have to try."

Her grandmother stood from the table and walked to the doorway. She grabbed her heavy coat off the hooks and looked back at Damon. "If you won't go that is your choice, but Ansley and I are leaving now. Ansley, come on." She turned and opened the door.

Damon heaved a heavy sigh and stalked toward the door after her. He looked at Ansley as he passed and mumbled only for her ears, "This is a bad idea. We will regret leaving your home on this night."

A chill passed over Ansley at those words, but she nevertheless grabbed her recently discarded shawl and repositioned it on her shoulders. She stepped back out into the night and glanced up at the bright stars winking again from above. "May the stars guide us." She whispered to herself, remembering the old prayer her father used to offer to Kius, the god of night, before embarking on a difficult task. Ansley closed her eyes and pictured her father. In her mind's eye, she could only see him lying on that floor, bright blue eyes wide open and unseeing. Ansley gritted her teeth and followed her grandmother. She wouldn't let her father down. He deserved justice, and so did all the families that had suffered as she had.

***

Kenna stepped gingerly on the dead leaves, easing her way into the brush as silently as she could. She had lost track of Dane what seemed like hours earlier, but she knew he was up ahead, trying to find any traces of their quarry. Kenna had never dreamed that they would be chasing the attackers through the night. Especially in these mountains. *How did Dane even know that they were here?*

These mountains were notably the largest on the continent, with Hugo's peak reaching 19,381 feet. She knew that when daylight broke, she would be able to see it somewhere in the distance. The darkness hung so heavy on her now that she could barely see two footsteps in front of her.

She made her way quickly and quietly, hoping that they were somehow close to the attackers. Kenna also hoped that *they* would be the ones doing the tracking this time, and that she and Dane hadn't been led here into a trap.

***

Bianca led Damon and Ansley through the woods at the bottom of the Dream Hollow Mountains until she found the path to Otto's Point. It was a well-worn path that had been traveled often by those farmers living in Terra when the river had swollen and sent them to higher ground. Fortunately, the path seemed a secret that only elder dreamwalkers remembered. Damon's descriptions from the vision matched this side of the mountains, so she had simply started and hoped to stumble across some clues. She smiled to herself as she hastened a glance back at her search party. Ansley's breaths were short and quick, and her granddaughter frequently slipped on hidden roots under the brush.

Damon wasn't fairing much better. He followed closely behind Bianca. Despite her usual kind nature, she had decided to take a more direct and difficult path through the woods. It might have taken her more effort to step over each and every root that she anticipated to be in her path, but it was worth it to hear Damon cursing every time he fell or snagged on something hidden from view. She was an ally of his, but she didn't have to take it easy on him.

After a few miles, Bianca had eventually run out of terrain to challenge Damon. Trees gave way to hedges, and eventually the hedges became scattered. They could see straight in front of themselves for miles up the incline to Otto's Point. Bianca touched the quiver of arrows and her trusty bow slung over her shoulder. She hoped she wouldn't need it, but it was smarter to have it than to be caught by surprise by a predator.

She moved on in the darkness, closely followed by Damon and Ansley and still eager to find justice for her family somewhere on the rising mountains.

***

Kenna turned and stopped when she heard feet crunching the leaves to her right. She knelt down until her nose was at the level of the hedges, obscuring her from view. Then, a hand grasped her shoulder tightly, and she let out a gasp.

"Shhh." Dane said softly. "There you are. I've been looking for you *everywhere*. I found a trail. They are doubling back toward Greenwood falls, and I think I lost them." He frowned in frustration.

"Well, now what?" Kenna asked uncertainly. She wanted to keep searching, but dawn was only a few hours away. Chasing an enemy in daylight was not something Kenna was prepared for.

"Let's look around this area for another hour or so, and then we can stop for the night. If we don't find anything, we can continue on to Terra after resting. Maybe the elders will have more information. I can't believe we lost them after being *so* close," Dane muttered to himself as he stalked off to Kenna's left to continue searching for clues.

Kenna stood from where she had squatted in the hedge and began moving forward again. She could see that the sky had begun to lighten already. Kenna stifled a big yawn as she stepped forward and found herself plummeting towards the earth. She was at the bottom of a deep hole in the ground that had been concealed by dried leaves and branches. When she had hit the bottom, she had heard her ankle crack. Kenna whimpered in pain but distracted herself by glancing around for a way out.

The pit had been dug recently. She was surrounded by the large leaves that had concealed the pit from view. Kenna cursed under her breath. It had been a trap after all. "Dane!" she yelled toward the surface, hoping that he was the only one to come to her aid.

She was relieved when his head almost instantly popped over the pit. "What happened? Are you hurt?"

"I twisted my ankle, and I can't stand on it. But Dane, we have to get out of here! This has to be a-," Kenna's voice was cut off by Dane turning behind him to find someone standing there…waiting.

"Wait!" Dane started, lifting a hand in surrender, but the person lifted a shovel and hit Dane across the face before he could finish. Dane tumbled into the pit and landed heavily, nearly on top of Kenna. Kenna scrambled out from beneath him while trying not to move her ankle. She gingerly touched the spot on his head where blood flowed freely. Kenna glanced back up to where Dane had stood only moments before, but the person had disappeared. She looked back at Dane's unconscious form in utter defeat.

***

Bianca continued walking. They had changed directions once Damon found an old trail that seemed to be heading to Greenwood Falls. She hurried along at a steady pace, noting how much strain it put on her aching joints. Bianca sighed. Even though she had known that the ceremony would age her, she didn't think it would come on so fast.

Ahead on her left, Bianca heard a shout. It sounded like a woman. She turned and looked at Damon, who instantly locked eyes with her.

He stared blankly in her direction before going rigid and falling to the ground. "Damon!"

Ansley and Bianca dropped their packs and ran to Damon's aid, but it was useless. He lay sound asleep on the ground, apparently pulled into the dream by an unknown tether. Ansley and Bianca shared a look before settling into the brush to await his return. Bianca could only hope that what he saw would help them reach the guilty party.

***

Kenna wasn't sure what had happened. She had been sitting on the soft earth in the black pit cradling Dane's bleeding head only moments before. Now, she found herself in a dream. She wandered around in the darkness. Had she been pulled into this dream or had she entered it herself?

A figure appeared to her left. The person was very far away from her, but as he drew nearer, Kenna could begin to make out his features. Her heart seemed to stop as she faced the person approaching. Bile rose in her throat.

"Kenna?" Damon asked in surprise. "What are you doing here? How did I get here?"

"Damon?" Kenna began breathing hard and fell to her knees as anger pulsed through her. Damon ran over to her, which was the wrong decision for him. He pulled her by an arm to her feet, and Kenna slapped him hard across the cheek, leaving a red mark. Damon reeled and faced Kenna with resignation.

"I guess I deserved that, but now isn't the time. I'm a bit busy at the moment, and I'm sure those with me in the mountains won't appreciate that I just collapsed into a useless heap. Can you spare me your reproach until we have more time?"

Kenna blinked twice in confusion. "You are in the mountains? Which mountains?"

"The Dream Hollow Mountains. We are moving towards Otto's Point."

"I should have known you were involved in these attacks!" Kenna exclaimed.

Damon's face turned white with anger as he spoke through his teeth, "Despite your opinion that I am the worst person alive, I am actually involved in helping my people."

Kenna paused for a moment, staring at him, before she said, "Too bad you couldn't do that last time." Damon shook his head at Kenna. Kenna finished, "My friend and I need help. Do you think helping two strangers is too much to ask of you?"

"Tell me where you are," Damon said frustratedly.

TWENTY-TWO

Ansley

Damon gradually lowered the rope into the pit. He had one end tied around the nearest tree trunk to prevent from dropping the unfortunate travelers once they started to climb. Ansley looked anxiously toward her Nana, who was standing opposite to her and holding onto the rope. She then looked down into the pit to determine what was happening, but the darkness masked any signs of movement.

"Okay! Here he comes!" A female voice yelled back to them after tugging twice on her end of the rope. The rope went taut as someone began climbing. It wasn't long before a man emerged. His skin and hair were dark, and he had a dazed look in his eyes. Ansley noted the blood matting his hair on one side. She guessed that he had hit his head when he fell and retrieved her canteen for him. Damon and Nana each grabbed one side of the man and heaved him over the ledge that had begun to crumble under his scrambling hands. He rolled onto his side and sat slowly, reaching his hand to his temple to assess the damage. His amber eyes were glazed in pain.

"Is she able to climb?" Damon asked. Ansley turned her head in confusion.

"She has an injured ankle, so it may take her some time," the man replied as he accepted the canteen of water from Ansley. He nodded in thanks and took a long draw from it. Ansley hastened a look at her grandmother. Her face betrayed her confusion as well.

Damon looked into the darkness below and said, "We are ready when you are! Let me know if you need us to pull you up."

No answer was made in reply, but Ansley could hear grunting as the woman began her climb. Ansley glanced to the sky that was mostly obscured by the foliage above. The sun was still hours from rising, and she had lost all hope of finding the attackers at this point. Ansley couldn't help but feel a sense of loss and despair as she waited quietly for the rescue to be completed. She glanced again at her grandmother and wondered if she felt the same. It had only been a few weeks since her family's death, but Ansley had felt such hope at the thought of bringing justice to their attackers. Though she had no guarantee that the ones they had been chasing had been connected to the man found in their barn only days before.

She shifted her thoughts back to their current situation as the woman began to emerge from the pit. She was older than Ansley, but still young. Her hair was dark brown and fell just below her shoulders. Blood was smeared across her face, but under it, her skin was tan. Her eyes were a striking green and emanated strength.

Ansley moved closer to offer a hand to the woman. She gladly accepted it and pulled hard, sending Ansley off-kilter. Ansley set her feet and pulled back until the woman was climbing over the ledge. The woman's ankle was swollen but not bleeding. She favored it and hobbled as she moved away from the dark edge. Bianca offered her an arm, and the woman leaned heavily onto her. They moved together until the woman was leaning against a nearby tree to catch her breath.

"Thank you," she panted. "If you had not helped us, we could have been there for days. I doubt this area is highly traveled."

She wiped her hands on her pants and looked around at all of them. Her gaze settled on Damon at last as he walked near her to untie the rope from the tree trunk. Her face immediately hardened, and her eyes seemed to turn to fire.

Damon seemed frozen for several minutes as he returned the woman's stare. Ansley felt uncomfortable from the tension she sensed between them. She looked at her grandmother for direction, but Bianca merely shook her head at Ansley and moved toward the man still sitting on the ground with Ansley's water canteen.

While Bianca examined the man's injuries, the tension seemed to subside between the other pair.

Damon addressed the man without speaking about the awkwardness that had just taken place between him and the woman, "What happened? And why are you here?"

"We were looking for our friend," the man said quickly. A little too quickly for Ansley to let go of her suspicions.

"Friend? Well, where *is* he? Is he the one who gave you that?" Damon asked while pointing to the man's head.

"I fell in the pit as we were walking, and then someone hit Dane as he tried to help me. He fell in, and the man ran off in that direction," the woman replied as she pointed to the east. The deepest part of the Forest of Visions. Damon sized her up with his dark black eyes, but the woman did not shrink against his gaze as Ansley often found herself doing.

"Well, should we keep looking for this…*friend* of yours?" Damon asked the pair, focusing his glare on the woman leaning against the tree.

"I'm done for the night. He can fend for himself," the man replied as he pushed himself to his feet. "Let's get out of this gods-forsaken place."

Bianca raised her eyebrows at the man but moved to pick up her pack. "We live south of the Dream Hollow Mountains, just a few miles from here. You are welcome to stay with us until you are ready to travel again."

The woman limped over to Bianca and extended her hand. "I'm Kenna of the Fischers of Willow."

Bianca smiled as she grasped her hand in return. "Bianca of the Blacks of Terra, and this is my granddaughter, Ansley. I would introduce you to *him*, but I sense that you two already know one another," Bianca said as she gestured towards Damon. He tensed his jaw in reply but said nothing. "So, I'm assuming you are also a dreamwalker, Kenna?"

Relief lit Kenna's face as she nodded. "Yes. We are actually trying to reach Terra. Is it near here?"

"Yes. Ansley and I live in Terra. We will provide you shelter until the council is available to attend to whatever brings you here."

"Thank you again for your help. We will gladly accept your offer. I am in *great* need of a soft bed and a hot bath," Kenna replied.

"We are all *exhausted*. I suggest we rest here an hour before making the trek. It will make it harder for you to walk, if you don't," Damon said, motioning toward Kenna's leg. From the limited light, Ansley could see how swollen her ankle was.

Kenna looked down and merely nodded, turning away from Damon. She propped herself against the tree again and sank to the ground.

"I'll keep watch first," Dane told the group, grunting as he touched his bleeding head again.

"Are you sure? You look like you need to rest too," Bianca asked gently.

"Yes. I've read about head injuries, and it is best for me to stay awake. Well, until we know if it is serious."

Kenna rolled her eyes at Dane's comment and caught Ansley staring in her direction. She shook her head at Ansley before closing her eyes.

"Suits me," Damon said as he laid on the bare ground and closed his eyes.

Ansley and her grandmother took off their shawls and arranged them on the ground. Within ten minutes, all were asleep.

***

The sunlight broke through the trees, and it gently warmed Ansley's cheek. She could see the sun through her closed eyelids and had a difficult time re-calling where she was. Her sleep had been dreamless because of her exhaustion from the day, but that hadn't stopped her mind from centering around Rhys as she slept. Even now, she could see his face smiling at her, but nothing had disturbed her sleep last night. She smiled as she thought of the last time she had seen him, and then she opened her eyes. Ansley immediately re-called the events of the previous night. At once, she knew something was wrong.

Ansley glanced around at the others who were still sleeping. Kenna leaned against the tree with her chin touching her chest, and her grandmother and Damon both lay on the ground breathing slowly. *Where was the other man?*

Ansley sat up and looked around but saw nothing in any direction. She stood quickly and moved to her grandmother, shaking her shoulder to wake the old woman. Her wrinkles seemed more pronounced as she slept, but maybe Ansley's eyes were playing tricks on her. Her grandmother opened her eyes, and Ansley moved to Damon, calling his name first. She didn't even make it near him before he sat straight up.

"We shouldn't still be here," he said softly. He turned to Kenna who was also now awake, face full of concern as she grasped her swollen ankle. "Where is your friend?" Damon asked her loudly.

"I don't know. He wouldn't go off like this. Especially when he is keeping watch."

"I wonder if someone took him," Ansley said, mostly to herself, but Damon heard her. He whirled back on Kenna. "Where is he!"

Kenna's concern vanished from her face, and her expression turned to stone and fire. She looked back up at the man standing over her. "If you want to know, maybe *you* should go look yourself, instead of *yelling* at me."

Damon stormed off into the brush. Bianca and Ansley began packing the blankets, and Kenna rose from her seated position to help.

"I hope he is okay," Bianca said looking at Kenna.

"I do too, but somehow I worry that *they* got him."

"*Who* got him?" Bianca asked in her most sincere voice, trying to draw some answer out of Kenna. Kenna shook her head as she stood on her uninjured foot with her back still against the tree trunk.

"How do you know…" Ansley started, but her grandmother waved a hand in her direction to quiet her.

"You know who we were *really* looking for out here because it was likely who you were looking for too." Kenna looked knowingly at the old woman.

"Take me to your council? We will need their help if we are ever going to find Dane," Kenna said with a defeated tone. Bianca nodded silently before calling for Damon. He appeared instantly, his face full of fury. Then the group began the trek back to Terra.

Ansley wondered how these strangers could have possibly been looking for the same group they had been searching for. *Who were these people, and why had they traveled to Terra?* Ansley shook her head in wonder as she followed the rest of the group back towards her grandmother's house. She wondered if they would ever find Dane.

TWENTY-THREE

Eight years earlier…

Everett sat in his chair by the fire as Ansley settled onto the couch with a pillow under her head.

"Daddy, it's late. Do we *have* to train tonight?" Ansley complained.

Everett leaned over and put his hand on his daughter's hair. "Yes. There are some things I need to talk to you about without your brother listening. Tonight's training is more of a history lesson and less of an adventure." His voice was solemn, and Ansley grew worried of what he might mean. She turned enough to take in her father over her right shoulder. She gave him a questioning look, but he sat silently rocking in his chair. The floorboards squeaked and filled the empty space in the room. Ansley knew that her mother and Ryker were both sleeping.

Everett sighed and finally said, "Ansley, have you heard us speak of the Black Night?"

Ansley nodded slowly and replied, "Of course I have, but I already know what happened. Surely this isn't another lecture on the dangers of telling typicals what we are?"

Everett shook his head and said, "No. There is more to that story than I wanted to tell you when you were younger. But now you are older, and you are training. You should know the truth." Ansley's eyes widened as she sensed fear in her father for the first time in years. She remained quiet, listening avidly as Everett continued.

"Terra *was* attacked, and the dreamwalkers were all targeted. As you know, the typicals came into their homes at sunrise and killed them. What you didn't know is that they first took their skills from them." Ansley let the information soak in.

"But Dad, there were hundreds of dreamwalkers murdered that night. Are you really saying that it was all to take their skills, rather than a hate crime?" She asked. Everett frowned. Ansley guessed it was at the thought of his ten-year-old daughter understanding what a hate crime was.

"Yes. That's what I'm saying, Ansley."

"But how? And *why* would they do that to us? It's not like they can use the skills," she said angrily.

"Actually, they can, Ansley. That's the hardest lesson our ancestors learned after that attack. The typicals had stolen skills before from lone dreamwalkers and used them to understand where most of the other dreamwalkers resided. When they realized the sheer amount of skills that existed in Terra, they attacked. We still don't know exactly how, but we do know that those skills were lost to us forever."

Ansley lowered her gaze at the fire blazing before her in the fireplace. "Is that why we have so many families with only a few skills available to pass on? Is it why so many of the others will never inherit?" She asked softly.

"Yes, Ansley. Our skills are finite. Once stolen like that, they can never be replaced," Everett responded as he turned slightly and glanced out the dark window to his right.

The room was silent for a few moments. "So, why did you want to tell me? Why *now*? I can't change the past."

"Ansley, you need to understand something about us. We may be blessed by the gods and have mighty skills in dreams, but they will not protect us in reality. Even though you may feel like it, you are never safe here. Or anywhere for that matter. I want you to remember that every time you decide to take a risk out there," he said, gesturing towards the window. "I am your father, but I can't protect you from everything, and someday, I won't be able to protect you from anything. I just want you to prepare yourself and understand that there are people who would seek to harm you because of what you are. Not just out of hate but because they want your skill for themselves."

Ansley nodded, trying to understand everything her father had just shared with her. She continued to watch the fire ahead as Everett rocked silently in his chair. They sat like that for hours until Ansley fell asleep. She hadn't realized it until the morning, but her father had carried her back to her bedroom and laid her in her bed. She was thankful he would always be there for her. As long as he was around, she need not fear the world like he had suggested.

***

Present Day

When they arrived back at Bianca's house, the group split into two. Ansley and Damon went off in search of the council members, and Kenna and Bianca settled in the kitchen to tend to Kenna's swollen ankle. Before Ansley had left, she spotted her grandmother pulling out a large map of Arvenia.

Ansley tried to hide her curiosity with Kenna's past, but it proved difficult. She couldn't help but be wary of a woman who shared a secret history with Damon. As the pair made their way towards Alden's cabin, Ansley turned in her saddle on Sal to look over at her trainer, who was riding her grandmother's horse.

"Who *is* she?" Ansley demanded of him.

Damon raised his dark eyes to glare at Ansley and then shook his head at her as he spurred Bill on to pass her.

"Well?" Ansley added, doing the same to keep pace with Damon.

"I don't know who you think you are, but I don't owe answers to anyone. And if I did talk to *someone*, it wouldn't be you." He kept his eyes ahead, and his tone was cutting. Ansley pulled Sal's reins to put some distance between them, and they rode silently as the sun rose higher above them.

Ansley continued at the distance for some time. Finally, she decided to spur on Sal to catch up with Damon, but then she felt a tug on her consciousness. Almost as if she was drifting away, Ansley closed her eyes. She forced them open again, but the tug was too strong for her to resist. She closed her eyes.

***

Ansley faced a brick wall in a windowless room. Shackles hung from the ceiling. The floor was made only of dirt, and several tables were scattered about. The tables were covered in dangerous looking instruments. Ansley stepped closer to the brick wall, where a dark shape dangled from chains.

Light flooded the small space as two large men pushed past Ansley to reach the dark shape ahead. The shape called out in pain, and Ansley was shocked to see a young man in front of her. One man grabbed a syringe from a nearby table, and the restrained man lifted his head to reveal a familiar face. Etched in pain and streaked with bruises, dirt, and blood.

Rhys saw through his torturers and looked only at Ansley. "Help me. Please, gods above, *Ansley. Save me from them." His voice whispered into the corners of the dark room. The men ignored him and plunged the syringe straight into the large vein at the side of his neck, sending him reeling backwards with a scream upon his lips.*

Ansley gasped and reached desperately in his direction..

***

Before she realized what had happened, Ansley was sitting once again in Sal's saddle, eyes open and staring at Damon's horse only a few feet ahead of her. Her breaths came quickly, and her heart pounded in her chest. "Damon!"

Damon slowed Bill and turned in the saddle as his horse stopped. His face betrayed his annoyance. "What is it, Ansley?"

"You seem like you have things in control. I think I will be more...*useful* helping Kenna and Nana." She tried to keep the emotion from her voice as she waited anxiously for Damon's reply. He simply shrugged his shoulders and turned Bill back towards Alden's cabin. Instead of responding, he spurred the horse and took off in a trot. Ansley leaned down and patted Sal on the neck.

"We have to go, buddy." She whispered into her old friend's ear. He seemed to sense her mood and took off instantly at a brisk pace. "Not quite fast enough, Sal," Ansley said to the horse, and she pushed him into a gallop. *Thank the gods that father taught me how to ride*, Ansley thought to herself. She reached for her bow and arrows slung across her back, and the feel-ing comforted her. She focused her attention on putting as much distance between Damon and herself as she could. She didn't want him to be able to stop her.

Rhys's blood-stained face occupied her mind. Determination filled her body. Ansley set out in search of danger, knowing that her father was at least watching over her now from the stars at night. She sent him a whisper and looked up to the sun-filled sky before lean-ing heavily against Sal's neck to urge him on even faster. His hooves made the only sound for miles across the fields of Terra.

TWENTY-FOUR

Rosalie
482 years ago

Rosalie sat down in the chair across from her son, Rael. Rael was thin and tall with straw-colored hair that fell to his shoulders. He was built like his mother. However, Rosalie had found that he possessed the same spirit that had drawn her to his father when she was young. At this moment, Rael's eyes were wide. Rosalie could still make out their deep brown color in the darkness of the cave, the same eyes as her late husband's.

It had been eighteen years since the Black Night, and she had finally found peace. Rosalie had raised her twin sons, Rael and Magnus, in the mountains. It was time to test Rael's training. She had seen this moment in her dreamvisions, even before the boys were born. Rosalie had never had the chance to share that she was expecting with Stephen. She despaired for many long nights after the events that stole her husband from her loving embrace. She wondered if it would have changed anything that had happened that night, but she knew better than most that the future can be undone with any decision. Even a small one.

Rosalie lowered her gaze from Rael to the knife held in her slender hand. She slid the blade gently

194

across her palm and then did the same to Rael's. He was as still as a stone, unflinching despite the bite of the blade.

"Are you ready?" Rosalie asked Rael. Rael swallowed his fear and nodded to his mother.

"Magnus?" Rosalie whispered, reaching her hand back toward the darkness. A hand reached out and took the used blade from her, replacing it with a short piece of rope.

She took in the boy's expression. In contrast to Rael, Magnus's skin was tan from spending his time in the sun. He preferred working in the garden next to their mountain home over spending time studying with his brother. Magnus's hair was cropped short and was as black as the sky during a thunderstorm. His blue eyes were dark and deep like the Glass Sea to the north of the Dream Hollow Mountains. Rosalie noted the disappointment on his face, as she said, "Magnus, it cannot be helped. I know no other dreamwalkers here, so Rael must inherit my skill. You will remain typical until we can find someone willing to part with theirs."

Magnus lowered his head and nodded. He stepped back into the shadows and let his mother continue the ceremony. Rosalie was saddened that Magnus would not be able to join his brother in inheriting a skill, but skills were of a finite number and not as readily available since so many had been stolen from her people during the Black Night. She turned back to Rael and said the words, clasping their hands together.

"I, Rosalie of House Black, acquired, used, and now I freely pass on. My skill belongs to my family."

"I, Rael of House Black, acquire. My family's skills are now my own."

He helped her tie the rope around their hands, and Rosalie felt a strong force almost breaking her in half as her skill left her body. When she could breathe once more, she knew that the inheritance ceremony had been successful. She felt an empty chasm inside. Her hands trembled as she looked down towards them, gradually accepting the change that had taken place.

Rael now sat across from her with his eyes moving rapidly beneath his eyelids. His breathing quickened as he began his trials. Rosalie lowered herself from the chair to a small cot laid out on the floor. Rest would be essential for her to regain what strength she could after parting with her skill. A shadow fell across her face, and she lifted her eyes. Magnus stood over her with the blood-covered blade held above his head. Darkness filled his blue eyes, and she found a new terror in them that she had never seen before. Instead of love, she found herself reflected in eyes full of disgust and hate. The blade plunged downward before she could reach out to Magnus, and Rosalie was encased in darkness.

TWENTY-FIVE
Ansley

Ansley thought it was odd to be setting out on a rescue mission in the midday light. Nevertheless, she pushed on her steed, turning him west towards Avendale. She urged Sal on and held onto the reins. Her fingertips turned white from her tight grip. Ansley's mind raced ahead faster than Sal's feet, which were pounding out a steady rhythm below her. She hoped that they would make it in time.

Ansley had no idea where they were going, but she felt a tether in her chest to Rhys and followed it. Every few moments, that tether would pull her in a slightly different direction. She would adjust Sal to match that pull. She should have asked Damon about this. They had never talked about how to find the source of dreamvisions, but somehow her heart just seemed to know. Ansley leaned forward in the saddle and spoke softly to her trusty chestnut friend.

"Fly Sal. We must *fly*." She gave her favorite horse an encouraging stroke of the neck, rustling his beautiful black mane, before returning her attention to the source of that pull on her mind.

***

It had been four grueling hours, and Ansley had finally arrived. Or at least, she thought she had. She had settled Sal in a nearby clump of trees to conceal her arrival at the small storehouse on the outskirts of Avendale. She had almost forgotten how long it took to reach the city from her family's land. Ansley had lost track of time as Sal had carried her further and further west. The miles flew by as her thoughts settled on that never-ceasing pull from her inner compass.

Sal had galloped past farmhouse after farmhouse until the world grew wild once more. The few miles from the outskirts of Terra to Avendale had been left unfarmed, and all sorts of plants and wildlife had overtaken the land. The soil in this area had been deemed hard and stubborn. Not suitable for growing the many vegetables and herbs that were sent during harvest to support Avendale.

As they had neared the outskirts of the city, Ansley had turned Sal from the gravel path of the road in favor of the brush and cover of the forest. She had ignored the few travelers who were out this time of day, bringing their wares to the city. Several small shops lay outside the borders of the city, and these shops were known to carry the most expensive goods available from Terra to Willow. Her father rarely, if ever, stopped at one. He said that it wasn't worth being cheated on the pricing. Instead, he traveled the extra few miles into the city. All of this was quieted in Ansley's mind today, as she focused solely on the compass leading her and Sal.

Now alone and on foot, Ansley inched along the outside of the building toward a nearby window. She peered inside and saw only her own reflection in the glass. She ducked her head below the windowsill and eased herself into a sitting position, leaning against the weathered gray bricks of the storehouse. She guessed that the building had once stored grains and produce brought in from Terra for the people of Avendale to purchase. It now stood abandoned and eerie. Ansley took a deep breath and closed her eyes. She traced that tether in her mind to this spot. *Yes, this is the right place. They must be holding him in some unseen room or lower level, but why had he even been taken?*

Ansley calmed herself and checked the position of the sun. It looked like she had a little over two hours until sunset. She would make her move with the cover of darkness.

She dug her hand into the bag slung across her back and pulled out a wrapped package of foods. She had grabbed it before their last trip into the mountains to find the attackers. *Gods above, that had been only the day before.* It seemed like time was dragging its feet and stretching itself into years or decades. She anticipated the worst outcome of all the so-called *adventures* she had endured over the past few weeks. What she wouldn't give for a normal existence again.

She felt a tear sliding down her cheek and angrily wiped it away as memories of her family filled her mind. Ansley pushed these aside and tried to focus on Rhys instead. He was her *closest* friend, and she couldn't fail him. Ansley chewed on the stale bread and waited for her moment to strike.

***

After the last of the pinks and blues in the sky had faded to black, Ansley stretched out her legs and pulled her bow off her shoulder. She nocked an arrow neatly in the bow and stood from the ground, stalking her way towards the door. The door opened with a loud creaking that would have easily betrayed her presence to anyone paying attention. Thankfully, nobody came to investigate the noise. She closed the door as quietly as she could manage. Her eyes adjusted after several blinks to the darkness inside the building.

Ansley rotated on the spot, careful to move her arrow along with her eyes. Nothing. She spotted another door in the corner of the building and a stairwell across from her. Aside from that door, there was nothing here. *Except* for a few small shapes that were moving quickly along the floor. Ansley swallowed her disgust and tried not to look too closely at them. She moved, poised with her bow, towards the door. With one outstretched hand, she tried the doorknob, but it was locked. Ansley turned sideways, silent on her feet, and placed her ear against the metal door. She listened for several moments before deciding that nothing was inside the room of interest to her. She looked instead in the direction of the stairwell. *Down.* She knew she had to go downstairs.

The stairwell was wooden and creaked under each foot she placed. Ansley hissed under her breath. If only Damon had given her a lesson in stealth along with her other lessons. She stopped counting the steps when she passed the fortieth. *How far down do these stairs descend?*

The air grew cool and moist as she stepped down and found herself standing on a dirt floor. This immediately reanimated Ansley. She lifted her bow which had relaxed a bit from its ready-to-fire position. She saw the shackles hanging from the ceiling just like she had seen in her dream, and there were steel tables along the brick walls. She noted almost instantly that these tables were empty of the tools she had seen before. She paused for a moment, looking at the ground below the shackles. There was blood, but it was not fresh. It looked like more of a stain than a recent addition. Sudden movement startled her, causing her to jump slightly. She rotated immediately and raised her bow to aim.

"*Ansley?* What are *you* doing here?" A man standing almost six feet tall addressed her. He had dark wavy locks and deep blue eyes. He stood half in shadow, but she could make out a face etched in confusion. *How did he know her name?*

"Who are you?" She demanded, her tone dripping with venom. "*Where is he*?"

"Where is *who*? How did you find me?" The man asked as he started to walk towards her. Ansley took a step back and aimed for the man's right eye.

"*Stop!* I asked you a question! *Where have you moved him*?" Her heart was beating an angry rhythm in her chest, but her practiced hands held steady on her weapon.

"*Ohhh*." A grin crossed the man's face as he ran his hand through his hair thoughtfully. "Of course! You don't recognize me."

In confusion, Ansley lowered her bow tip towards the floor.

"It's me, Ansley. Rhys."

***

They ascended the stairs Ansley had taken such effort to descend moments earlier. She was surprised to see that such lush existed behind the locked metal door. It hid a cozy office with several large, cushioned chairs. Rhys offered Ansley a seat as he lit candles on the table.

"It gets so dark here at night," he said as he shook the match's flames into smoke. He smiled warmly at her. His nose was smaller, and his face was thinner than the one she had seen so frequently. Stubble also grew on his chin, which was dimpled instead of pointed like it appeared in her dreams. As he sat across from her, she found that all she could do was stare.

"You must be wondering *why* I look so different. It's not a pleasant story, I'm afraid," he said, smile fading from his lips. "I was in a hunting accident a few years ago, and the damage done to my face left me looking like a monster. I had no choice but to seek expert healers to try to fix what had been damaged. This is the result of their experiments."

"But….there are no scars," Ansley said quietly.

"Correct. They are experts and work specifically to prevent scars in their patients. I was lucky to find them and even luckier to be allowed to pay off my debt to them slowly. They demanded a huge sum that my father and I could not afford."

Ansley looked again at his face, which was no longer handsome or warm. She wondered if those characteristics had been taken from him in the accident as well. A smile spread across his face once more as he said, "But why and *how* are you here?"

"I had a dreamvision of you." Ansley paused for a moment, trying to choose words to reflect her feelings about the vision. "You were…dying, and I knew you needed me." Ansley swallowed as the images of Rhys in chains came back to her. Then, she opened her eyes and looked back at the unscathed man in front of her. "I am so glad you are okay. Maybe my visions do not always come to pass." She added softly.

Rhys's smile froze and melted away like the snow under warm sunlight. A bit of his color faded along with it. "You saw my *death?*"

"Yes. I had to try to save you. Thank the gods you are alright ," Ansley said while reaching for his hand. He gave it to her and squeezed her fingers gently. "But what are *you* doing in a place like this?" she said, gesturing behind her towards the main room of the building. At that moment, a loud noise echoed through the empty storehouse. Their conversation paused. They both turned and looked at the closed metal door.

"It must be an animal that has come in. I'm sure it's no cause for alarm," Rhys said. "Yes, this is a dreary place, but it was my father's. It has been abandoned for the season to begin adding improvements to its design. I try to check on it often to keep thieves out. I saw a horse tied to a tree nearby when I was going toward my home, and I thought I should investigate. That's how I found you here."

"How did you know I was down *there?*"

"You weren't quite as stealthy as you thought you were," Rhys said, smiling once more. "But come, let's go to my home instead to acquaint ourselves. This is the last place I had hoped to meet you for the first time." Rhys stood and blew out the candles as he ushered Ansley out of the extravagant but also musty office. They walked to the old entrance and heard that loud noise echoing through the empty storehouse once more. Ansley's eyes found Rhys. He was staring at the stairwell.

"It's nothing that can't wait until the morning. Let's go. I'm sure you haven't had dinner, and I am *famished*." He held the door open for Ansley and followed her outside in the crisp night air.

After they left, the clanging of metal continued, followed by unending cries made throughout the night. All which went unanswered.

TWENTY-SIX

Kenna

Kenna leaned back in the stiff chair and gingerly stretched her ankle out under the table. Bianca had bandaged it and said that the swelling was from a twist of the joint and not a break. Kenna had been relieved. She crossed her arms and glared at Damon. He was standing on her left and leaning over the kitchen table. They had marked sites of known attacks on the map of Arvenia. She had helped with places surrounding Willow, and Bianca had handled most of the areas around Avendale and Terra. The map looked like a bullseye, with pins sticking out of many places surrounding the center. They were surprised to find that the center of the attacks seemed to fall within a 15-mile radius around Bianca's son's abandoned farm.

Damon had insisted that it was not a coincidence, but he had no evidence. That grimy traitor had led their discussions throughout the day, and he took the lead on any plans regarding future actions. Kenna frowned and wondered how Bianca could trust someone so *foul* to be under the same roof as her and her granddaughter. She tried to keep her opinions to herself, though. Damon had arrived back at Bianca's house alone. Both women questioned him about Ansley, and Damon seemed confused as well.

"She said she was coming back here, but maybe she stopped along the way?" He had offered. As to Alden's absence, Damon had told them that the old man had insisted on rounding up both Daro and Quinn before arriving at Bianca's house. He was troubled by the events and determined that it needed the attention of the full council of Terra. Kenna attempted to pull her mind back to the conversation.

"…coming around dinner to discuss their findings with us. Alden insisted that we not be hasty in any decision-making until they arrive. Every hour that passes could lead Dane further away from us. It would be best to strike fast, while we are more likely to find them," Damon insisted, slamming his fist on the table for emphasis.

"Them? We don't even know who *they* are!" Kenna added. "Don't you think this whole thing is absurd? Dreamwalkers attacking other dreamwalkers…for *what*? They obviously already have skills of their own. It isn't as if we are dealing with typicals here. They also seem to have a pattern they are following, which, contrary to *your* thoughts," Kenna gestured towards Damon, "we have no idea about."

Bianca sat down in the chair poised behind her and exhaled. "You aren't wrong. But what about Dane?" She asked as she looked at Kenna. Kenna noted the growing abundance of grey hairs that now peppered

Bianca's head. She wondered how they had appeared almost overnight.

"What about him? Obviously, it is very important to find Dane, especially since he is one of my tribe, but he knew the risks in coming here. He decided to come anyway, and now he has been taken. Should we really risk more lives when we don't even know where to look?" Kenna countered. She brushed her dark hair behind her right ear and stood from her chair. "We need to think. We can't rush into anything without risking more deaths or injuries. We do know that they attacked us in the mountains, so we have some sort of lead there. They knew that Dane and I were following them, so they tried to get us off their trail. Maybe taking Dane was their way of assuring we would leave them alone." Kenna stood behind her chair and shifted her weight off her injured ankle. She winced and remembered how Edric had not wanted her to leave Willow. *If I wasn't here, someone else would be. Better me than someone who may get killed in the process,* she speculated.

Bianca turned to Damon, who remained silent. He scratched the stubble now covering his chin, as if debating a new idea.

"We don't have any other choices, do we?"

"What do you mean?" Bianca asked, confused.

"I mean that you need my skill, and I will have to find Dane for us."

"How would you do that? You can see visions but that doesn't help us if you aren't seeing what we need you to see," Kenna spat. She calmed herself and rolled her shoulders once to relieve tension before adding, "It will only put you in unnecessary danger."

Damon's lip curled at her words. "I would think that you would be okay with that, *Kenna*." His black eyes bore into her before he let his smile fade. "It may be dangerous, but it *is* necessary. I will prepare, and we will do it after we meet with Alden."

"What do you need?" Bianca. Ever the gracious host.

"I need to join Kenna's tribe," Damon sighed.

"What? Why would you *ever* think I'd allow that?" Kenna growled.

"Because I am our only shot at finding Dane, and your tribe is the only one we know of that has had direct contact with any of these attackers. I need your memories to locate them. If we simply bind ourselves together, the link will not be strong enough."

Kenna sat down and covered her face with her hands. She shook her head slowly thinking of the message she had sent to Edric earlier. She had not told him that the seer helping her was Damon. Not that his name would mean anything to Edric. He had never met him or heard her speak of him.

"Fine. But let me speak with Jameson first. As our leader, he has the final call," Kenna said into the hands covering her face.

"I'll be outside when you are ready." Damon turned towards the door.

***

After a short meeting with Jameson during an afternoon nap, Kenna went in search of Damon. She had tried to dissuade Jameson from agreeing, but he had reminded her that this investigation had been her idea. Jameson had also reminded Kenna that if a solution could not be found quickly, Dane might be killed. Kenna had relented on this note and inquired about the other members of her tribe.

Laurel was healing but skittish about returning to dreams with the others. Edric had been taking turns with Jameson to keep watch over her at night to ensure she wasn't attacked again. Sophie had put her talents to use in trying to identify any potential victims. So far, the group had been unsuccessful. Five other dreamwalkers were targeted. None had survived.

With this stark realization, Kenna knew that Damon's plan would have to be followed. She just hated knowing that he was the one to lead it. She also hoped that his former personality traits would not emerge in the middle of their mission: dishonesty, disloyalty, and a duplicity that tended to get all those around him killed.

Kenna walked around the house but did not see Damon anywhere. The sun was starting to set in the west, and the horizon was filled with smears of blue, fuchsia, and orange. Kenna stopped, letting go of her frustration to admire the sunset. She wondered how something so beautiful could appear at such a time of crisis. Shaking her head, she continued past the barn towards the empty fields.

She saw Damon sitting up ahead with his back against a tree trunk. He had some type of herbs burning on a log in front of him, and his eyes were closed. From the rapid movements beneath his eyelids, Kenna knew he was dreamwalking. She approached him silently and sat in front of him in the soft grass.

He continued on for several minutes before he let out a sigh and opened his eyes. He immediately focused on her sitting in front of him and said, "Nothing. No matter how hard I try to find *something,* I only find nothing." His black eyes betrayed little emotion other than anger. She saw it simmering beneath his surface and wondered when it would erupt.

"Well?" he asked, leaving the question between them.

"He agreed...rather quickly. It seems that my own opinions have no place in the discussion anymore. Five more dreamwalkers have been killed on the coast. Who knows how many more will be lost before this is finished?" She stood from the soft earth and brushed the residue from her worn brown pants.

"Kenna, I've been meaning to say- "

"Leave it. We don't have the time, and I don't have the patience." She said curtly as she turned and walked slowly on her tender ankle back to the house.

"Come inside. This won't take long."

***

Bianca and Kenna cleared the table and pulled out two chairs that were seated side-by-side for Kenna and Damon to use. The materials needed for a tribe initiation were always made in the dreams. Kenna's tribe was a small one, and their ritual was simple. Only about fifteen or twenty minutes. If they timed it right, they would be finished before the council came.

"I guess we are all set," Kenna said. She noted the look on Bianca's face. "What is it?"

"It's just...Ansley still isn't home. She usually isn't away this long without sending word. She should be back by now." Bianca glanced out the window towards the west as if she sensed something bad had happened to the girl.

"I'm sure she just lost track of time or got lost trying to find her way back. Let's finish this quickly, and if she isn't back by then, I will help you look for her."

Bianca nodded silently and sat down in a chair on the other side of the table. Damon sat on Kenna's right and offered his hand. She looked down at his out-stretched hand and noted the dirt under his fingernails before looking at Damon's face. His unrelenting glare met hers. In the quiet space of her mind, Kenna hoped that he had had a hard life. She let out a breath. Damon did too, as if sensing the thought that had passed through her mind.

"Let's get this finished," Kenna said as she clasped hands with Damon and was instantly pulled into a dream.

***

Kenna walked into the small house and found Jameson and Sophie standing by the winding staircase. They both approached Kenna and hugged her.

"We were so worried!" Sophie said. "Edric has been strong, but I know he is missing you terribly." She stepped back, and Kenna saw a tear trickle down Sophie's cheek. She was surprised by the uncharacteristic show of emotion. Sophie reached to wipe the tear away. "It has been hard without you both."

Kenna touched Sophie on the shoulder before turning to Jameson. "Where is Laurel?"

A shadow passed across his face. "She hasn't been willing to dreamwalk since she was attacked, but I think she will recover her courage in time. Come, let's start." Jameson gestured into the room, and Kenna led their group through a small door into an open space that looked like one reserved for assemblies.

Damon followed closely behind Kenna, who introduced him to her tribe. Both Jameson and Sophie shook his hand. Many candles had been lit in the open space, and the door was closed to provide darkness for the initiation. Jameson picked up an ornate silver cup from a long table. He held out in his other hand herbs for both Sophie and Kenna to take. They selected their favorites and waited silently.

Jameson began. "We, of House Fischer, have made a place for you in our tribe, Damon. Drink from the cup and join your skills with ours." Jameson added his herb to the cup. He passed it to Sophie, who crushed her mint leaves before sprinkling them over the rim. Sophie then handed the cup to Kenna. Before she added her blooms of lavender, she glanced at Damon. His eyes were soft and warm. Her cheeks grew hot as she dropped her herb into the cup and passed it to him. Damon nodded and drank deeply.

After he had drained the cup, Jameson took it from him and turned to Sophie. Sophie approached Damon and shrunk in form to that of a young girl. Damon's eyes widened with recognition. He took in the young Kenna standing before him in surprise.

"Damon, do you accept all past responsibilities and promise to redeem yourself moving forward?"

Damon had lost his voice. He simply nodded in response. Sophie stepped back, returning to her own form. Nothing was said between the tribe members about Sophie's choice of appearance, but Kenna was touched that Sophie had chosen to demonstrate her loyalty to Kenna by choosing her childhood form. She had shared all of her history with her tribe, but she had never expected them to take up her battles. Nevertheless, it was nice to feel like she had a family again.

Jameson nodded at Kenna, and she stepped forward to challenge Damon. She lifted her hands and felt the earth crumble around them. Her anger was channeled into her skill, pulling the earth into many large cracks in the floor. Jameson had to jump to escape a fall, and Damon teetered on a narrow island, surrounded by empty air on all sides.

"Damon, do you pledge to honor your tribe and sacrifice all to protect us, even your life if needed?" Damon stared at her, but he quickly found his voice and said, "Yes, I do so pledge."

Jameson nodded at Kenna, who then moved her hands above the rifts in the floor to form a bridge between Damon's tiny island and the uneven floor where the others waited for him.

"Damon, if you are ready, you may join us," Jameson said.

Damon stepped onto the bridge hesitantly and walked slowly forward. Upon reaching Jameson, he knelt. Jameson removed a dagger from his robes and cut a small wound on his arm. Jameson marked

Damon's forehead with the constellation of the Fish by dipping his finger in the blood bubbling from the cut.

"Rise, Damon, and join your tribe." As Damon stood, the group was released from the dream.

***

Kenna took a deep breath and looked over to Bianca who gave her a questioning look. Damon opened his eyes and answered for Kenna, "It is done."

TWENTY-SEVEN
Ansley

Outside the storehouse, a black mare was tethered to a tree next to Sal. They were happily munching on grass when Rhys and Ansley approached.

Rhys untied his horse's reins from the tree as he said, "Let's go into Avendale before we go to my house for the night. It is just a short ride from here, and my house is an hour further to the south. I am starving, and I'm sure you are too." He smiled again at Ansley, flashing those sparkling, dark blue eyes.

"Wait. I need to send word to my grandmother. She is probably going out of her mind with worry." Ansley thought guiltily about Nana, brushing her hair behind her ears.

"No need. Send her a dream message," Rhys said.

"A *what*?" Ansley asked, frowning.

"A dream message. You haven't heard of them?"

Ansley shook her head in response before pulling herself onto Sal's back, her bow and arrows neatly slung across her back once more.

"Here, I'll help you. First, close your eyes. Then, go into a dream. Find your tether and use it to pull her in. You can tell her what you need to say."

217

He must think I am a child to not understand such concepts. "But what tether?" Ansley asked stubbornly.

Rhys smiled at her graciously. "Look for it. It will be there. We are all tethered to our family members, especially those who give us their skills."

She sighed and closed her eyes, obeying his instructions.

"Breathe in and out. Focus on where you want to go." He said to her. She felt Sal's muscles move beneath her as he shifted to reach for more of the grass.

***

Ansley stood on her own feet. She looked around in awe of how quickly she found her way into her own dreams. She supposed it helped that dreamwalkers need not be tired.

How to pull Nana in? She thought. "Nana?" She called. Nothing. "Nana!"

Several moments passed, but nothing happened. Ansley stood in what appeared to be a dark room with nothing around her. Well, she wasn't a wielder, was she? She wondered what it meant to "pull" someone. Thoughtfully, Ansley closed her eyes and searched within her mind. Curiously, she found a tether there, much like the one that had brought her to Rhys. How could she be sure it was the right one? There were several others around it. Choosing to trust her instinct, she tugged on that thread and waited.

"Ansley?"

Ansley opened her eyes in surprise to see her grandmother before her. "It worked!"

"Ansley? Where are you? I was so worried! You can't run off like this while dreamwalkers are being attacked." Her grandmother's eyebrows furrowed, and her lips pursed. Ansley had expected to see this reaction, but she was not a child anymore. She felt her cheeks grow warm from her grandmother's scolding.

"I'm sorry, Nana. I never meant to scare you, but someone was in danger. I had a dreamvision, so I came to try to help him."

"Who? Are you alright? Why didn't you tell me where you were going?" Bianca demanded angrily, her eyes widening.

"Yes, but I am very far away. I'm in Avendale, and I won't make it back before the sun rises. I was worried if I told you where I was going, you wouldn't let me leave," Ansley replied, standing her ground.

"You were right about that! I've already lost my son. I will not lose you too."

"I miss them too, Nana, but you can't keep me away from the world. These visions are given to me for a reason, and I must use them to try to help others! I won't stand by while innocents die!" She felt the thread pulling out of her mental grip, and her vision grew blurry.

"Ansley! Wait!" Her grandmother called as the dream faded.

***

"Well?" Rhys asked with a questioning look.

"It worked. Let's go," Ansley said, trying to shake her residual anger away. She would deal with her grandmother later.

***

Ansley and Rhys rode together down a narrow dirt road with a row of trees lining each side. The stars glittered beautifully above and winked at Ansley as she followed her mysterious companion. They talked as the miles passed, and Ansley found that he was the same person she had met in her dreams. He smiled and laughed with her as they talked of happier times in their lives. Then, he began telling her of the history of the lands they rode through. Ansley found herself yawning.

"Tiring of my history lessons?" Rhys asked playfully, his eyes sparkling like the stars above them.

"It has been a long night. Or day, really," she replied softly.

"We are about half a mile from the city," Rhys offered. "I haven't found your dreams for the past two nights. Have you been alright?"

"Not particularly."

"Do you want to talk about it?"

"It's a bit of a long story, Rhys. I don't know if I want to subject you to the horrors I have been through lately," she answered. It may seem to him like a dramatic comment from a teenage girl, but in honesty, it was the truth.

"Well, let's finish our journey, and we can talk about it on the way back, if you wish." Rhys reached out to Ansley and grabbed her hand gently. "You are not alone, Ansley. Not anymore."

She looked into his face and found only sincerity there. Ansley nodded and turned to face the lights of the city that were approaching in the distance.

***

Once they reached Avendale, Ansley followed Rhys toward the gates and finally dismounted Sal. They led the horses to a watering station that was by the entrance. A boy ran up to Rhys, and Rhys traded two silver coins in exchange for a small piece of paper. He handed it to Ansley, who turned it over to find two numbers on the back: thirty-six and thirty-eight.

"Those are their stall numbers. They will feed and water them for us while we eat. Come on. Let's find something you like," Rhys said as he walked away from their horses. Ansley patted Sal one last time before following Rhys down the cobble-stone road.

There were lamps on both sides of the road. *Electricity.* She had heard that Avendale had the latest technology, but she had never been here to see it. Turning to see what kept her, Rhys smiled at her wonder and grabbed her hand to urge her on.

They passed store after store of clothing, food, and goods. Ansley suddenly felt the urge to gaze down at her own attire. Her light brown leather pants were worn and had small holes in various places where she had caught herself on the sharp fences around her family's land. Her once-white linen top was now spotted with brown dirt smears from earlier in the day when she had wiped her hands before eating her bread. Ansley glanced up and saw her reflection in the glass pane of one of the stores. Her hair was braided but pieces stuck out, creating a disheveled look. Her face felt warm, and she reached up to her hair.

Rhys saw this and wrapped an arm around her shoulders. "Don't worry about that here. It is the dead of night, and no one worth knowing is out. We are here to recover from a long journey. No one expects to see a rider come in so late looking any different."

Ansley nodded in response as they entered the one inn that had lights burning at this hour. There were small round tables filling the room, and a warm fire burned in the corner, providing extra light. A portly man approached them. "Room and board?"

"No thank you. Just dinner and a wash," Rhys replied to the man.

The man nodded taking a handful of Rhys's silver coins. He gestured behind him to an open door near the kitchen. "In here, if you will."

They stepped inside and found a large basin positioned on the one table in the room, various types of soaps, and running water. *Wow.* Ansley thought to herself. *I wish we had these on the farm.* She stepped forward to examine the basin and the metal spout positioned over it. There were tiny little levers that she assumed turned on the water. She could hardly imagine what it must be like to wash and even bathe with such ease. Ansley had always had to draw water from the well for baths.

When the man had left the doorway, Rhys said, "Come find me when you are finished. Take your time." He smiled warmly to Ansley while he closed the door behind himself.

She took the soap and washed her dust covered hands and arms, spending extra time cleaning under her fingernails. *Ladies should be clean and sparkle like silver.* She heard her mother's voice echo in her mind. Ansley swallowed her emotions down before turning her attention to her braid. She unwove her hair and ran clean water over it. She chose a lavender soap and added it to the water before dipping her hair into the basin. Once she had washed and rinsed a second time, she wrung the extra water from her hair before deftly re-braiding it.

Ansley hastened a look in the mirror at her reflection. Much improved from before. She stepped out of the washroom to find Rhys, feeling a rumble from her stomach as a smell of freshly cooked beef beckoned her to a table nearby.

***

Rhys and Ansley ordered a meat pie, fresh vegetables, and ale to wash it down. Rhys had almost fallen off his stool when Ansley had attempted to order water. He hastily shook his head and whispered in her ear,

"Not here. Ale is the only halfway suitable drink in places such as these." He leaned back and a small laugh escaped his lips. Ansley smiled at him before saying, "Ale it is then."

They ate heartily before leaving the cozy inn to venture back into the streets. The moon still hung in the sky with no hint of the sun's arrival. Although she had been tired before, Ansley found herself invigorated from her meal. They walked the length of the street to inspect the windows of each store and inn before turning back to the barn to retrieve their horses.

Once they were in their saddles and riding back on the tree-lined road, Rhys said, "So, tell me your story."

Ansley took a deep breath. "We've talked about the attacks in Terra, but I didn't tell you that my family was one of those murdered." She paused and looked at Rhys, hesitant to continue.

"Oh Ansley, I am so *sorry*," Rhys replied, sadness lining his face. "When did it happen? Is the murderer still at large? I know there have been other attacks in Terra."

"It happened last month. We did find the man responsible, and he is dead. I know that the ones responsible for planning it are still out there. Our council fears it is a dreamwalker, or group of dreamwalkers, that are attacking all of our people."

Rhys's eyes widened, and they rode in silence for several moments. "How *could* they…" He started angrily. "How *could* they betray their own?"

"That is the worst part. I have no idea why they would target my family. They were all so good." Ansley choked on her tears at the last word, covering her mouth to hide the emotion beginning to pour out of her.

She launched into the whole story with Rhys, telling him about the need to find the murderers, her hurried inheritance ceremony, and her fast-paced training. Tears fell down her face as she confided in him all the burdens that had been placed on her. Rhys listened quietly before pulling his horse's reins to move closer to Sal. He reached up and stroked Ansley's face.

"You are not alone. I will help you however I can, Ansley. I am so sorry you have had to deal with all of this," he said before gently stroking her cheek with his hand.

Ansley eyes closed, taking in not only his words but his promise. She let out a long breath and felt the world tilt beneath her.

***

Ansley found herself inside a small house. She anxiously looked around the room, trying to understand how she came here. It all seemed so familiar, but she couldn't quite place where she had seen this scene before.

Just then, she heard a familiar voice.

"Ansley?" Josilyn asked quietly. "What are you doing here? I haven't invited you into my dreams." Josilyn's golden hair was pulled away from her face into a braid. Ansley thought it made her look like she was just a child again. Her green eyes shone brightly, but no smile lit up her face.

"Wait, I've been here before," Ansley said as dread filled her. "Josilyn, are you okay? We have to get-," Ansley trailed off as Josilyn suddenly disappeared once again, just as she had in the original dreamvision. Ansley turned and looked around the kitchen in confusion.

"Josilyn!" But it was no use. Josilyn had disappeared from the dream once more. Ansley turned in circles screaming her friend's name as her vision became blurry again...

***

Ansley felt a hand shaking her shoulder and firm ground beneath her back. She opened her eyes to see Rhys leaning over her.

"Ansley, are you alright?" His face was lined with worry.

"What happened?" She asked, reaching up to touch the back of her head where a sharp pain now stemmed.

"Don't," Rhys replied, trying to encourage Ansley to lie still. "You were talking and then suddenly stopped. By the time I looked over, you had fallen from your saddle. You must have hit your head hard. What did you see in your dreamvision?"

Recollection shook Ansley. "Rhys, we have to go to Josilyn. She is in danger."

Rhys looked confused as he helped Ansley to her feet.

TWENTY-EIGHT

Bianca

Bianca sat at the table, boiling with anger towards Ansley. She tried to quiet herself by sipping on a cup of coffee. Kenna and Damon continued to glare at one another from across the table. *What was their story?* It must be something heavy to cause such damage, but she put nothing past Damon.

A knock on the door pulled her out of her reverie. She rose and found Alden, Quinn, and Daro standing in the darkness. She held open the door for them to enter and murmured greetings to them as they passed.

Alden shot a wary look in Damon's direction before sitting at the head of the table. Then he turned to Kenna and said, "I don't believe we have met. I am Alden, lead elder of the council of Terra."

Kenna stood, bracing herself on the table, and bowed to the man. "I am Kenna of the Fischers. I have come from Willow for your help. Our dreamwalkers are dying. Actually, let me rephrase that. They are being *murdered*. We have watched silently for too long, and finally, my tribe sent my companion, Dane, and me to seek your council."

"Where is this…Dane?" Daro asked looking around the small kitchen at both Bianca and Damon.

"He was taken," Damon offered.

Quinn's eyes widened at this information. "Is he dead?"

"Not yet. I can still feel his tether to our tribe. My tribe members have confirmed this observation. Dane lives. For now," Kenna replied staring boldly at Alden.

"Yes, for now, but who knows how long that will be. We must find him. Do you have any leads? We have experienced similar crimes in this area," Daro added, looking meaningfully at Alden.

"In this family," Bianca confirmed softly. All members of the council bowed their heads in reverence to her statement.

"All we know for certain is that these attacks are connected. There has been a symbol marking where they have been. At every place someone was attacked, a circle with an arrow below it was found. What does it mean?" Damon asked.

Alden's silence filled everyone. Behind his silver-rimmed glasses, his eyes had a knowing look to them. He tugged anxiously on his short grey beard and finally said, "This is an ancient cult that I thought had gone out of existence. It appears they were only waiting for another opportunity to strike."

Quinn and Daro turned to Alden as if questioning him. Bianca sensed a hesitancy between the pair, as if they were trying to urge Alden to remain silent. Alden continued, "I knew after I saw the symbol at the sight of Bianca's son's murder that there was a possibility of the cult being restored. There is only one record of their existence, and it is from around five hundred years ago. It was recorded in a diary of one of the survivors of the Black Night. An ancestor of yours, Bianca."

A hush fell over the room as understanding swept among them. Bianca felt a chill pass over her.

"That is impossible. It *can't* be the same cult." Damon said, shaking his head. "These are *dreamwalkers.*"

"How do you know that?" Alden countered. "Have they told you so? Have you even seen them *yourself*? Have any of you?"

"I have," Kenna said. "They attacked my tribe. That is what compelled my tribe to send me here."

"Well, were you convinced of their skill?" Alden questioned her, his grey eyebrows rising.

"I thought so, but they never used those skills in the dream. They chased me and tried to grab me. I could have been mistaken."

Alden turned silently to Damon, as if proving to him that what he had said was true. Bianca finally realized that her knuckles had turned white from gripping the back of the chair she was standing behind. She released the wood and drew in a shaky breath.

Alden continued. "In the diary, these cult members used that same symbol. Sometimes it was even seen as a brand on the forehead of the cult's members. The diary is considered a reputable source."

"Are you saying it was typicals before? Typicals that orchestrated the Black Night?" Bianca asked.

The elders shared a look before Daro replied solemnly, "That is what our ancestors believed, but it was never proven."

The room was silent for a few moments before Damon finally spoke. "Well, what do we need to do?"

"We still do not know much about these people. We need to find where they are hiding so we can bring them to justice," Daro replied. Alden nodded in agreement with his brother.

"Damon, you know what to do," Quinn said. Her statement was matter-of-fact, void of any emotion.

"Is there no other way?" Damon asked, his black eyes glistening with fear.

"I think you owe your council this one favor. *Wouldn't you agree?*" Alden posed. His anger smoldered like a fire, and Bianca was surprised to suddenly remember his anger in Everett's barn.

Damon nodded silently. Bianca became thankful that Ansley had not been in the house to hear this discussion.

TWENTY-NINE

Ansley

Rhys helped Ansley to her feet. She had a large bump on her head. Thankfully, she wasn't bleeding. They mounted their horses and raced in a new direction-east-as the sun pulled itself up over the horizon. Ansley felt that she was racing time itself as Sal galloped across the farm fields of Terra. She took in the scenery illuminated by the streaks of light that hit the ground around her.

The wildflowers were strewn everywhere, like someone had tossed a handful of seeds into the wind. White, red, yellow, pink, purple, and orange dotted the rolling fields. Many of them were trampled under the horses' thunderous hooves. She turned her head to the right to glimpse at Rhys on the black mare. He had called her Serena, and she did look serene as she galloped beside Sal. Ansley hoped that the horse would be able to keep up with them as she urged Sal on faster. She could see his hot breath in the cold morning air as his legs pumped them closer and closer to Josilyn.

She found herself once again hoping that she wouldn't be too late.

***

Ansley waited, but no one answered her knock on the door. She turned toward Rhys and nodded, a silent signal for him to open the door. He unsheathed a small dagger at his belt and used it to pick the lock. Finally, the lock clicked and the door swung inward.

Ansley entered carefully and quietly. She instinctively pulled her bow from her shoulder and notched an arrow before making her way into the kitchen.

Upon turning the corner, Ansley spotted someone lying on the floor face-down. Ansley felt her heart stop as she took in Josilyn's fanned blonde hair. She rushed forward and gently flipped her friend over. Josilyn's eyes were closed, but she was breathing. Rhys crouched beside Ansley. He studied Josilyn before saying, "She is sleeping…" His bewildered look made Ansley's heart stop once more.

"What should we do?" She whispered.

"Let me check the rest of the house," Rhys said before leaving the kitchen.

He returned several minutes later to find Ansley where he had left her. Ansley brushed Josilyn's hair gently away from her face and turned to Rhys.

"I need to see what is happening to her in there," Ansley said tremulously, her voice cracking with worry for her friend.

"Then go." Rhys replied.

Ansley's mouth fell open before she said, "Will you not come with me? I may need back-up."

"I can't. I haven't been invited," Rhys said.

"I forgot. You're right. I will be back as soon as I check it out," Ansley whispered. Rhys grabbed her hand once more, locking eyes with her.

"Be careful in there, Ansley. You don't know what is waiting for you."

Ansley closed her eyes and fell into her friend's dream. She found it odd that she could enter Josilyn's dreams, but her grandmother had once mentioned that the girls used to dreamwalk together when they were children. Maybe Bianca was right, and she had been invited without remembering.

***

Ansley opened her eyes to see Josilyn's kitchen just as it had appeared before she had entered the dream realm. The only difference in the scene were two people sitting on both sides of Josilyn, holding her arms down.

"Stop! What are you doing?" Josilyn screamed at the man and woman sitting on either side of her.

"Hold her tighter," the man growled at the woman. Ansley noted the strange circle on his forehead. Was that an arrow below it?

The man touched the ground, and roots ripped through Josilyn's wooden floors. The roots lifted themselves like arms and wrapped themselves around Josilyn's wrists and ankles, pinning her down.

"There. Now we are ready," he said again to the woman. Josilyn struggled against her bonds, crying hysterically.

Ansley gasped as the woman pulled a necklace from her pocket. A thin black cord ended in a white crystal. She placed the crystal in the man's hand.

"Shut up, girl!" The man screamed at Josilyn, who whimpered in reply.

This was bad. This was really, *really bad. Ansley knew that whatever that crystal was, it was not something that would help her friend. She rose to her feet, preparing to make a move, but then she saw the man hold the crystal to Josilyn's forehead. Josilyn screamed louder, and a bright light etched itself on her forehead where the crystal touched. The shape glowed brightly, illuminating the dream, and Ansley noticed that it differed from any mark she had seen before. This mark was in the shape of an animal with the head of a lion, a serpent's tail, and wings.*

Realization hit, and she touched her own forehead. That was Josilyn's mark. A shifter's *mark.*

The mark glowed brightly before the crystal began pulling that same light away from Josilyn's mark. Her screams echoed, and Ansley gasped once more as she realized her friend's face was aging. Small wrinkles appeared around Josilyn's mouth, and a strip of her hair turned grey.

235

Light poured into the crystal. Ansley had to do something. Now. She had no plan. She had no hope to beat them, but she ran forward in the hope that surprise would be enough. Ansley purposefully reached back for her bow and was pleasantly surprised that it had come into the dream with her.

"Hey! Leave her alone!" The pair turned to look in Ansley's direction. Shock lined their faces as they took in the bow leveled at them. Ansley aimed for the woman first, but she was too fast. The woman sprang out of range, and the man leapt for Ansley. Ansley began running backwards until her back hit the table. She notched a second arrow, aimed for the man, and let it fly.

A small cry echoed in the kitchen, and Ansley was pleased to see that the arrow had found its mark. The man reached towards his left shoulder, where the arrow had pierced his chest, and fell backwards. He dropped the crystal. The woman screeched and disappeared before Ansley could notch a third arrow. She hurried to Josilyn, who now lay with her eyes closed.

Ansley knelt down and picked up the black cord, careful not to touch the crystal. She pocketed it before releasing herself from the dream.

***

Ansley sat up and sprang toward Josilyn. She was uneasy upon finding that her friend still lay unconscious. Rhys instantly began peppering her with questions.

"Ansley, what happened? Are you alright? Were they there?"

Ansley touched the single strand of grey hair within the sea of gold. She touched her pocket before turning to Rhys, ensuring the crystal was still there. "We have to get her to the council. Will you help me carry her?"

THIRTY

Rhys lifted Josilyn onto Serena's back, and Ansley mounted Sal. They hastened towards Ansley's grand-mother's house. She explained what had happened to Rhys on the way, shouting details at him as Sal's hooved beat out a steady rhythm underneath her. Rhys listened quietly, but his eyes continued to widen with the information. The sun had risen, and their trek was passing by quickly. Ansley's thoughts were on Josilyn and the crystal housed in her pocket.

When they reached her grandmother's house, Ansley burst inside, quickly followed by Rhys. He car-ried Josilyn's unconscious form in his arms. Her arms dangled down to the floor. The council was seated around the table along with Damon and Kenna, finish-ing up a small breakfast. They all rose from the table in alarm.

"Ansley!" Nana started. "What has happened?" She paled at Josilyn in Rhys's arms.

"Nana, this is Rhys, the friend I was trying to save last night. I had another vision, while we were to-gether, of Josilyn. When we got there, she was dream-ing." Ansley relived the dream with the group, pulling the crystal from her pocket at the end, careful only to touch the black cord. Ansley noted the light that swirled inside the tiny crystal and realized in horror that it must be her friend's skill.

Alden moved closer to her. "Ansley, give that to me please." He held his hand out, and Ansley complied. Alden closed his hand on the crystal, but it didn't harm him. Ansley gasped. Alden turned to Rhys. "Put her on the table."

Rhys gently laid Josilyn's slight form on the wood. The others gathered around as Alden moved to the head of the table with the crystal in hand. He touched it to her forehead and whispered a sort of spell with his eyes closed. A bright light glowed from the crystal and eventually seeped back into Josilyn's forehead. The symbol Ansley had seen in the dream reappeared at last, glowing brightly to accept the skills being transferred. After the crystal was void of light once more, the mark faded from Josilyn's forehead.

Color returned to her face, and her eyes flickered open. "Ansley?"

"You are safe here," Ansley replied.

"You saved me," she breathed in response.

Alden put the crystal into the pocket of his worn trousers before resting his hand on Josilyn's forehead. Ansley saw that the wrinkles and grey hair had not vanished. "Rest, child. You are safe here with us."

Josilyn closed her eyes immediately and slept. Her breathing deepened until it found a steady rhythm. Alden closed his eyes for several seconds before opening them and addressing the group. "She will dream of pleasant things until she is ready to rejoin us. You are lucky you made it to us when you did. She was fading."

"What happened to her?" Ansley asked incredulously. "What is that *thing*?" She added pointing to Alden's pocket.

"That is a dreamstone. It is used to remove skills when dreamwalkers are ready to move on. Our skills are attached to our soul, so removing the skills removes the life from us." The others listened intently. "We also use them to prevent a community from losing skills when dreamwalkers are unable to inherit."

"So, you use them to *kill* dreamwalkers?" Ansley gasped.

"No. When someone is ready to give up their skill, they must first separate it from their soul. If the break has been successful, they may live many years still. Josilyn had never anticipated that she would give up her powers. She had not broken that link, so they took much of her life from her," Alden informed Ansley. He pursed his lips. "I think we have found their weapon. How did you get this? Wasn't this used in the dream?"

Ansley nodded fervently, eager to understand. "I took it after the man dropped it."

Alden nodded. "And you said your bow appeared with you in the dream?"

"Yes, but I don't see how this is important. Shouldn't we be worried about finding these people instead of dissecting every detail of their attack?" Ansley was frustrated.

Bianca quickly chimed in. "Ansley, seers don't *make things appear* in dreams. Alden is right to question this." She turned to the elder. "What does this mean, Alden?"

Alden's lips curled into a smile. "It means that Ansley is not just a seer. She also has the gift of transference. The fifth skill gifted to the dreamwalkers by Vito."

"*What?*" Bianca and Ansley responded in unison.

Damon crossed his arms and replied as if he was annoyed with them. "It means she can summon things into dreams or reality with her. Maybe even people after she learns how to wield the skill. It is rare and only appears in seers."

Alden nodded and added, "There are few dreamwalkers with this gift known to us, but the last one we knew existed was in the Black family hundreds of years ago. It could mean danger for you, Ansley, but we can learn more of this transference later. Let's focus on the main issue for now. This cult has grown even more dangerous to us."

"We must act quickly. This situation is worse than we feared," Daro said in a hushed voice.

"Yes. If we don't act quickly, they may target Ansley for her interference. You said the woman got away?" Alden asked.

Ansley tried to shift her thoughts to the question that Alden had posed, but the word *transference* echoed in her mind. She put the thought aside with difficulty and swallowed her questions as she responded simply, "She did."

"Well, then let us begin." Damon said softly. Ansley turned to him confused. She was suddenly struck by the pain etched in her trainer's face.

***

"*What* is he going to do?" Ansley asked her grandmother blankly.

"It's called *scrying*. Only seers can do it," Bianca responded promptly as she put together a meager meal for the group. It had been a few challenging days, and they were all in need of some nourishment before moving forward with the next step of their plan.

"But I don't understand. Why haven't you told me about it before now?" Ansley asked as she followed her grandmother around the kitchen.

"It wasn't something you *needed* to know. It's very dangerous, and it could potentially kill the seer who tries it."

Ansley shook her head as she helped lay out plates of bread, meat, and cheese for their companions.

"A better question is who is this *Rhys*?" Bianca asked after a few beats of silence. "And why is he in my house?" She gave her granddaughter a stern look.

"Nana, it isn't like that. Well, it's...a long story. He found me first, and he is a seer like me. He lives in...you know what? It doesn't even matter right now. What matters is that you don't seem to trust me with anything. How am I supposed to be an *adult* when you won't let me?" Ansley's voice rose slightly. Bianca wiped her hands on her apron and turned back to her granddaughter.

"Ansley, this is neither the time nor the place for this discussion. Try to remember what happened to your family only a few weeks ago. Is it so wrong for me to try to protect you?" She placed a hand on each side of Ansley's face and kissed her on the forehead. "Let's worry about this later. We have bigger issues at hand. Now take these into the sitting room before our guests attack each other out of hunger."

Ansley picked up the plates and moved into the next room, still shaking her head and biting on her lip.

"That girl will be the death of us all," Bianca whispered to herself. She filled a pitcher with lemon water and followed Ansley to check on the others.

***

After they had eaten, Bianca and Ansley cleared the sitting room of the remains of the meal. Then, they pushed the furniture back against the wall to allow a large empty space for everyone to sit on the floor. They didn't have enough space at the dining room table, and Bianca had insisted on a carpeted room in case anyone fell to the floor while being pulled into a dream.

Several cushions were handed around, and a large map was opened up on the floor in front of Damon. He sat opposite Kenna, while the elders sat with their backs propped against the furniture. All sat ready, if needed.

Rhys and Ansley hovered in one corner, and Ansley tried not to show her terror. She was glad when Rhys reached down and squeezed her hand tightly. He leaned down and whispered in her ear, "I'm sure he will be alright, Ansley." Ansley nodded and turned back to look at Damon, who was speaking softly with Kenna.

"Do you have a safe place we can do it?" He asked. The lines around his eyes betrayed his concerns for what was about to happen. Kenna nodded silently, and Damon nodded in return. Then, he turned and began addressing the room.

"Okay, we have already completed an important step," Damon said, swallowing hard before continuing. He tried not to allow the fear to show in his eyes like it had earlier. "Now comes the hardest part. Kenna and I will walk together, and I will scry for Dane. Once I have found him, we will come back to tell you where they are. Then we will proceed *on foot* to attack them."

"I think that we will have the advantage in going there if we go there in the physical realm. The crystals are more powerful and more dangerous to us in dreams," Daro added, looking at his brother Alden for confirmation.

"Yes, and we can summon other dreamwalkers, if you think it is necessary, Damon," Alden said.

Damon nodded his head before reaching his hands out to Kenna's. "Wait, what does *scrying* mean exactly?" Ansley asked from the corner. Damon let his hands drop before turning to face her.

"It is part of your gift, Ansley. It lets you search for things or people across great distances in dreams."

"Why is this our plan?"

"If we find Dane before they target us again, it gives us time. We need that to plan a proper rescue. At least one that will be successful," Damon said, turning back to face Kenna.

"And how is it dangerous?" Ansley added. Her grandmother turned to her to give her another scolding look. Ansley knew she was stalling him, but she needed to know. If this was something she could do too, she had the *right* to know.

Damon sighed and looked back at Ansley. "It is very difficult to do, and so it takes all of my concentration. As I continue to scry, it requires immense power. The only power I have that comes close to that need is tied to my lifesource. The longer I work, more of it is taken from me." Damon lifted his eyes to Ansley's, and she thought she saw something there she had never seen before. The blackness quickly devoured that trickle of sadness.

"So, it ages you, like the crystals did to Josilyn?"

"Yes, but faster," Damon said, sighing again. "Any other *questions* before we start?" He growled in her direction, trying to mask his true emotions.

"No. Walk well, Damon," Ansley said, touching a finger to her forehead in salute to him. She had never used that greeting with another dreamwalker, but somehow it seemed appropriate here. He stared at her for a moment before inclining his head to her. Damon turned back to Kenna and held out his hands once more. Kenna responded by placing hers over his without touching him.

"Are you ready for this?"

Damon did not respond. He simply lifted his hands to hers, and instantly, they were gone. Their eyes were closed, but they sat still as ever. Ansley observed their quick eye movements beneath their eyelids. She squeezed Rhys's hand.

"Now we wait." Alden said quietly to the group.

THIRTY-ONE

Kenna

*K*enna *and Damon found themselves on a familiar, quiet street in Willow and facing the ocean waves rolling in beneath the dock. Kenna took a deep breath and relaxed as the salty breeze filled her lungs. Damon glared at her.*

"Did you really have to bring me here?" He asked as they began walking down the street.

"You said we needed a safe place to work, and I thought this would be better than most. Come on, Damon. The last time you were here you weren't quite so glum*," Kenna said in a mocking tone.*

"I'm sure you would understand my distaste for the place if our situations were switched," he replied.

Kenna didn't respond, although anger burned in her chest. Now wasn't the time to harass Damon about the past. They needed this to work, and they had to work quickly. She led him down the street to her store and pulled a key from her pocket to unlock the door. The glass pane walls reflected the rolling movements of the sea, just as she remembered. As she followed Damon into her store, she was hit with smells of cleaning supplies and salted fish. They passed rows of fabric, cooking supplies, and jars of candy. She led Damon into the back where her office was located.

A cozy little room, her office boasted electricity and a small fireplace for those evenings when she had to wait for deliveries from the local fishermen. The air off the ocean could bite at times, and she always enjoyed lighting a fire in the hearth.

"Does this suit our needs?" She asked, spreading her hands to gesture around the room. Focused on the task ahead of him, Damon simply walked to the chair facing her desk and sat down. Kenna followed his lead, sitting opposite from him once more.

"So how do I help?" She asked softly.

"You need to picture Dane, seeing every detail you remember of him. Every little detail. I will use your memory to scry for where they are holding him," Damon instructed her.

"Will this really take your life, Damon?" Kenna asked, softening her voice.

"I hope not," he said, rubbing his chin thoughtfully. "Now, come on. Let's get to work." Damon put one hand on each side of Kenna's brow and looked her in the eye. "Remember, don't pull away from me. It isn't a pleasant process, and the pain may make me...unlike myself. Don't respond. Just let me work."

"Have you done this before?"

"Only once, and it lasted less than a minute."
Damon touched the streak of gray hair over his left ear.
"This is my badge of honor from that experience."

Kenna took a deep breath, finally understanding. She nodded and closed her eyes. "I'm ready."

She felt his hands on her brow once more. Then, an intense burning erupted where he touched her face. Kenna frowned but tried to remain still. Her thoughts settled on Dane and the night they had shared a meal in the inn. She pictured his clothes, his arrogant smile, and the glow in his amber eyes. She began to feel as if she was on a fast-moving horse, galloping through time. It had only been a few seconds, but it felt as if a lifetime had passed her by already. Then she started to feel herself move in circles, large circles. Her head began to hurt from the pressure Damon was putting on her temples.

She jolted as a lightning hot bolt erupted from his fingertips. Damon let out a growl, and she knew that it had really begun. She tried to stay still for his sake, but it felt like he had lit her face on fire. The combination of the burning and spinning had started to make her feel ill. Try as she may, she could not continue with her eyes closed. She hastened a peek at the man in front of her. What she saw horrified her. She gasped as she beheld the skin on his face and arms seemingly melting and rolling into wrinkles. His dark brown hair started to show spots of grey in the space of seconds.

"Don't!" He yelled at her, and Kenna quickly closed her eyes once more. She focused again on Dane and kept that picture firmly in her mind, reminding herself of the danger Damon faced if they made a mistake.

Then, all at once, the burning in Kenna's temples stopped. His pressure released, and she opened her eyes to find him lying face first on her desk.

"Damon?" She asked, timidly reaching out a hand to touch his back.

He gingerly lifted his head from the desk, and Kenna noted the smattering of wrinkles around his eyes and mouth. His hair had turned grey like the clouds before a thunderstorm, and his hands shook as he lifted himself to a sitting position.

"I found him," he coughed.

"Well, let's go back and get help," Kenna said, pushing herself from the chair and moving to help him stand.

"Kenna, I just wanted to say..." Damon began as she lifted him to his feet.

"Later, Damon." Kenna said soothingly. They stood together and closed their eyes.

***

Instantly they were back in the sitting room with eyes staring from all directions. Damon leaned forward and touched a place on the map with his forefinger.

"Here." Then, he turned to the side and vomited. Bianca was there in an instant to help him. She lifted a cloth and poured cool water over it from a nearby pitcher. She used the cloth to wash Damon's face as he gasped for breath. Kenna looked around at the others and saw the concern in Ansley's eyes as she beheld the changes to Damon's appearance. The elders, Ansley, and Rhys moved closer to the map to look at the location Damon had identified.

"That's impossible," Rhys said softly, standing over the map to inspect the spot on the map Damon had pointed to.

"What? Why?" Kenna asked, turning back to see Rhys's face, which had turned ghastly white.

"That's my father's storehouse. Nobody is allowed in while the repairs are made," Rhys said, almost in a whisper. His face was so pale that Kenna noticed the black circles under his eyes, as they widened in horror.

"What does this mean?" Ansley asked, turning towards Rhys first before turning to look at her grandmother. "We were there only yesterday. There was nothing there."

Rhys's face seemed to become even more pale. He made eye contact with Kenna, and Kenna felt the sudden urge to look away. Something was wrong here.

Kenna and Bianca looked at one another, sensing the change in the room. There was no time to discuss it. Kenna and Damon collapsed to the floor as they were pulled into another dream and the world around them vanished.

***

Bianca rushed to their aid but was unable to wake either of them. "What has happened?"

"They found us before we could find them," Daro said softly.

"We have to do something!" Bianca said. She turned Kenna and Damon onto their backs, and everyone gasped as they saw their marks glowing with light. "They are going to take their skills!"

"There is nothing we can do, Bianca. They are only here in the dream realm, and we cannot enter when we haven't been invited into their dreams. If they were typicals, it would be different," Alden said softly.

"This can't be true! What are we supposed to do? *Watch them die*?" Bianca gasped.

"Wait, I *was* invited. I was invited into Damon's dreams! We share the bond," Ansley said, stepping forward.

Bianca turned to her and shook her head firmly. "No. I forbid it."

"The girl may be their only hope, Bianca," Alden said. Bianca turned and watched the light glow brighter on the brows of the two sleeping walkers. She covered her face with her hands and sobbed into them.

Ansley gently touched her shoulder. Bianca looked up as tears ran down her cheeks.

"Nana, we have to act fast or it will be too late."

Bianca felt desperation fill her soul. She bowed her head in defeat and nodded.

"Ansley, can I speak with you privately for a moment? Please?" Rhys asked, stepping forward. Ansley and Bianca looked at him with confusion.

"Ansley? Please?" Rhys asked, extending his hand to Bianca's granddaughter. Ansley looked at Bianca once more and wrapped her in a hug.

"I will be back in a few moments, and then, I will be ready," she said as she released her grandmother. She left the room to follow Rhys outside. Bianca remained where she was, kneeling on the carpet between the two sleeping bodies. She glanced at the council and found three sets of eyes reflecting the fear she felt so strongly. Bianca shook her head as she covered her face with her hands once more.

THIRTY-TWO

Ansley

"I have an idea," Rhys said quickly. His minutes were numbered. "Have you heard of the blood oath?"

Ansley shook her head, and Rhys continued. "You are the only one invited into Damon's dreams, but I can help you from the outside if we use it. It links us together, and you can use as much of my strength as you need to defeat the cult members." His face seemed desperate and hungry, much changed from the way it was only the day before.

"What do we have to do?" Ansley asked, ready to do anything needed to save her trainer. Frustrating as he may be, Damon was the only one who could teach her how to use her skill. She needed him.

"Give me your hand," Rhys said quietly. He took the dagger from its sheath on his waist and cut a small line on her hand. Then, he lifted her hand to his mouth. "Repeat after me. One blood, one skill, one mind," Rhys said before touching his lips to Ansley's cut. She shivered from the feeling, but it was over in a moment. When she looked back at Rhys, he was wrapping her hand with a piece of fabric he had ripped from his shirt.

Ansley lifted Rhys's hand to her lips and said the words, "One blood, one skill, one mind." She touched her lips to the cut on his hand and gagged at the tangy, metallic taste. She forced herself to swallow, and almost instantly felt herself fill with power.

"Do you feel it too?" Rhys asked.

"Yes. Now let's go inside." She turned and led him back into the house as he wrapped his own hand in more of his torn shirt.

When they entered the room, Bianca's pained eyes found Ansley's. She motioned for Ansley to come to her. Ansley sat beside her grandmother. Bianca took Ansley's face into her hands once more and said, "You are a *Bear*. Not just any Bear, but a *Black* Bear. Your ancestors fought in battles hundreds of times worse than what you are about to do. You have their strength, and I know you will not fail." She kissed her grand-daughter's forehead a second time, lingering there for a moment before releasing her. "Walk well, Ansley."

The council echoed the sentiment, "Walk well, Ansley." They saluted her with a touch of their forefingers to their brows. Ansley nodded and closed her eyes, focusing on Damon. Then her surroundings faded around her.

***

Kenna's knees hit the earthen floor of the room hard enough to knock the breath from her. She leaned forward as she tried to understand what had just happened. She could hear Damon doing the same to her right. When she raised her head from the floor, she heard a familiar voice giving instructions.

"It worked! Get them now! Restrain them both. Especially her.*"*

Kenna's eyes blinked to become accustomed to the dark room. The room they were in looked like a cellar. Two sets of rough hands grabbed her arms and dragged her backwards towards a wall. She struggled but could not free herself from the strong grips of the men. They slammed her head into the brick. Kenna saw stars and gave up her fight. She was vaguely aware of them pulling her arms upward and a clicking sound.

When she was able to see clearly, she realized there were chains hanging from the walls. Her arms strained against the chains, and her feet barely touched the floor. She jerked forcefully but to no avail. Kenna spotted a small stone that lay on the ground and stretched her fingers in that direction, willing it to turn into a key. The stone did not budge. The chains must be keeping her skill at bay. Kenna turned quickly to try to warn Damon to escape, but it dawned on her that he was already hanging by his arms beside her.

"Damon?" She whispered anxiously, but Damon did not move. Blood trickled down the side of his face from his now-grey hairline. His knees touched the floor, and his eyes were closed.

"Don't bother. He won't wake. Scrying for us took too much of his energy." That familiar voice spoke

again, now directly to her. Kenna squinted and saw a man emerge from the shadows ahead. Kenna stared in disbelief.

"You had no idea, did you?" Dane smirked, tossing a rock against the wall. He reached up and rubbed his forehead until the mark of Orco was visible through whatever he had used to obscure it.

"What does this mean? Are you behind this?" Kenna gasped in utter disbelief.

*Dane laughed. "If you thought you were miserable traveling around with me for weeks, imagine how I felt! Traveling across the countryside with a know-it-all, like you?" Dane snorted as he walked closer to her. She could feel his breath on her face. "Watching you with your...human. Pathetic! I can't believe you settled for someone...*typical.*" Dane turned away from Kenna to welcome the others rushing down the stairs.*

"I need crystals. Bring me five." The men nodded and ran back up the stairs to retrieve them.

"It was you the whole time? You led them to Laurel!"

He laughed again. "Led them? My dear, I attacked Laurel myself. She couldn't see my face because I wore a mask," Dane sneered at her as Kenna's eyes widened in shock.

"How could you betray us?" Kenna spat, lifting herself to her feet by pulling on the chains holding

her wrists. "You joined our tribe and pledged to be loyal to us. To protect us!"

Dane smirked again. "I joined your tribe, and after I realized how pathetic it was, I decided to find a better one. That's when I found my real tribe." He gestured around himself to the men walking in behind him.

"You mean cult." Kenna said angrily.

"Cult? There are no such things as cults, Kenna. There are only groups of others who are more determined to succeed. Don't call us a cult just because you fear our methods. It is unbecoming of you. Should we be stopped because we want to see our leader rise in power? Because we take skills and give them to those who really deserve them? Or because you don't agree with how we go about what we are doing?" Dane asked. He walked to Kenna once again and ran a finger down her jaw.

"You are welcome here, you know. I could make sure that you are heartily accepted," he whispered in her ear. Kenna pulled her face from him and spat near his shoes.

Dane jumped back and cursed her. "Fine, Kenna! If that's how you want it. Don't worry, you'll join your precious family soon. But before then, let's have your tribe join you as well. We are always eager to find skills that are linked."

"Wait, you're giving the skills to others? Who?" Kenna asked, trying to distract Dane. She *watched as the other men unlocked the chains next to Damon's to prepare for more prisoners. She couldn't bear to see Jameson and Sophia there, let alone Laurel after what she had been through.*

"Who do you think? The ones that don't have any, of course. Dreamwalkers who weren't lucky enough to receive their family's skills and....typicals. You'll find that weakness leads to mindless support. Especially support for those who are strong enough to maintain it," he responded as he pulled up a chair to sit in front of her. Kenna cut her eyes at Damon, and she saw that he was beginning to wake up.

"He's a bit of a mess, isn't he?" Dane asked, gesturing to Damon. "For someone that is almost a hundred years old, I thought that he would be more impressive." Dane stood and walked towards Damon. "I guess scrying really takes it out of you, doesn't it, Damon?" Dane punched Damon hard in the stomach, causing Damon to gasp for breath. "That one was for you, Kenna. I hope you appreciated it. Didn't you say he was the one?"

"Stop it, Dane," Kenna said with her teeth bared.

"Stop? For him? I never thought you would ever forgive someone so despicable," Dane said mockingly. "He is the one who killed your father after all."

Kenna closed her eyes tightly trying to shut out Dane's words. But Dane continued, "Yea, so if I got the story right from Jameson, he met your mom, fell in love, and murdered your father. Apparently, the guy had such little self-confidence that he thought murder was the best option for him to ensure he got the girl. Wow!" Dane shook his head and laughed. "And here you are, working with him! You really are more senseless than I thought, Kenna."

Kenna risked a glance at Damon, and she thought she saw tears welling up in his eyes. "That's not how....it didn't happen that way..." Damon sputtered, still wheezing.

Dane moved closer. "What's that, old chap?" Damon took a deep breath and tried again. "It was an accident. Then Vida couldn't handle it. So she....she..."

"Yes, yes. We know. Well what's passed is past," Dane said and patted Damon on the shoulder. Damon let out a genuine sob. Dane looked down at his watch. "Look at that! The time for all this chit-chat has passed. Why don't we get down to business? You first Damon, you- "

But Dane didn't finish his sentence. Kenna was amazed to see Ansley, Bianca's teenaged-granddaughter standing over Dane with a shovel in her hand. Dane now cowered on the floor, holding his head in pain.

Ansley ran over to Kenna and tried the chains' locks. "It's no use. He has the key" Kenna said hurriedly.

Ansley leaned over Dane and dug through his pockets. Dane seemed only aware of the blood dripping *from the back of his head. "It's not here!" She shouted back at Kenna. "Why can't you make one?"*

Kenna shook her head. "I've tried already. There is something in these chains that prevents me from using my skill. We will have to find his key."

Several men and women came running down the stairs in response to Dane's roar of pain. They seemed surprised to see him on the floor. Only when they saw Ansley standing beside him did they seem to understand what had happened. Several of the men ran toward Ansley. Hands grabbed her from all directions, and the people shouted to one another.

"They have reinforcements!"

"...will ruin our plan!"

"Get her!"

Ansley was instantly overwhelmed, and with her capture the only hope for Kenna and Damon's freedom died. "Kenna! I can't...I can't!" Ansley shouted as she struggled. She closed her eyes for a few seconds, and Kenna was worried the girl was conceding defeat. Unexpectedly, Ansley wrenched her arms free and effectively threw all those holding her against the opposite wall in the cellar with strength Kenna had never seen before in a dreamwalker.

Kenna's eyes widened in response. Ansley had no time to explain before numerous others sprinted down the stairs for her. "Kenna! There are too many!"

Ansley screamed over the voices of their foes, shouting instructions at one another.

Kenna shook her head. What could she do against a number this large? She turned to Damon, who she was shocked to see staring at her. Blood continued to trickle down his temple onto his stubble-covered chin.

"You did not inherit, Kenna. You know *this. Even when you were an infant, your mother knew the truth. You are elite. With that comes strength," he whispered before spitting a mouthful of blood onto the already stained dirt floor.*

Kenna stared at him for a moment, shocked to hear her secret finally spoken aloud. Is that what she was? *Kenna turned away from Damon and closed her eyes. She searched deep within her mind. She dug down into the depths of herself and was surprised at what she found. A deep, unflinching power. She had never noticed that before, but why not? Maybe she had not needed it until now.*

Kenna pushed aside her thoughts as she immersed herself in that power. She imagined herself holding a piece of metal in her hands and twisting it into a meaningful shape. A key.

Kenna heard the locks break on her chains. She gasped in shock at what she had done and was equally surprised to see that Damon's locks had broken as well. He collapsed on the floor, still weak from scrying.

Kenna left him on the floor and raised her hands. Five people still trying to corner Ansley stopped to stare at Kenna in fear. One reached to his neck to grab a crystal much like the one Ansley had given Alden.

Kenna drew on her strength and shoved outward, causing the earth to ripple away from her. The five men and Ansley all fell to the floor. Kenna put her palms together and then pulled them apart slowly, breaking the dirt floor so that a chasm developed. Two of the men fell in, and she could hear them yelling from the bottom of the pit. Ansley scooted back to the wall and searched for something to hold onto. Kenna shoved outward again, causing another ripple in the earth. The staircase began to tremble. Screams were heard from above as the men and women tried to reach the crumbling cellar. Dane rolled onto his back and took in the chaos that was ensuing.

"Damon, Ansley, move!" Kenna said, calling over the sounds of the ceiling beginning to give way. Dust trickled down from cracks that tore into the floor above them.

Damon crawled forward and grabbed Kenna's leg. He gave her a squeeze to let Kenna know he was out of danger as Ansley bolted away from the wall. She made a massive leap across the chasm before landing short and barely managing to grab the ledge. Kenna paused her destruction until she saw Ansley pull herself up the small ledge and roll over the side. Once Ansley was safe, Kenna sent repetitive shock waves through the floor to the staircase. The entire building shook as if an earthquake had begun, and huge boulders began to fall from the ceiling above. One hit Dane, and he lay quiet.

Ansley dodged the falling debris and finally reached Kenna and Damon. She placed her hand on Kenna's arm. She asked as loudly as she could over the sounds of destruction, "Will it work?"

Kenna shouted in response, "Yes, but we have to lock them in the dream!"

Ansley looked at Kenna in bewilderment, but Kenna did not explain herself. She simply bent forward and used her finger to draw a circle around the three of them on the dirt floor. Once she had finished the circle, Kenna stepped inside, closed her eyes, and mumbled a few words in the elder tongue, the ancient language of the dreamwalkers. "It's ready! Let's go!"

With her command, all three dreamwalkers closed their eyes and pulled themselves out of the cellar. Kenna could hear the building collapse and the screams from those inside as she exited the dream.

***

Kenna opened her eyes and realized that she was once again laying on Bianca's carpeted floor. She turned and saw the others open their eyes as well, noting the cuts on Damon that he had sustained from the falling rocks. Kenna pushed herself up on her arms to look at Alden.

"You don't have to worry about Orco's cult anymore. They have been destroyed." Then, she let herself fall forward again, this time falling into a dreamless oblivion of needed rest.

THIRTY-THREE

Magnus
482 years ago…

Magnus stood over his mother's motionless body and exhaled sharply. He turned to face Rael, who still sat in the chair and engaged in some dream battle to achieve the goal of inheriting his mother's skill. Magnus stepped closer and waved a hand in front of Rael's closed but rapidly moving eyes. Nothing. Magnus quickly sat down in the chair opposite Rael and wiped the blood from his hands onto his pants. He used the knife to cut his own hand like his mother had cut Rael's and her own. Then he reached out and touched his cut hand to Rael's, hoping it would work.

***

Magnus blinked twice and found himself in the midst of a thick forest. Heavy brush obscured the floor, but Magnus could hear animal and insect noises all around. He glanced down at his hand and was disappointed to see he no longer held the bloodied knife. He reached up to the branches above and broke off the largest one he could, throwing his weight towards the ground. Then, Magnus removed all the smaller pieces on the branch and turned to search for his brother Rael.

Magnus knew that his brother would be surprised. He smiled maliciously while thinking of the look on his pathetic twin's face. How could she choose him *over me? Magnus thought to himself. She knew I was the stronger of us. They will both pay.*

Magnus slowed his pace as he approached the shadow of someone ahead. He focused on silencing his footsteps as he neared Rael in hopes of having an element of surprise.

Rael did not turn but instead, continued kneeling silently on the brush. Magnus heard him speak, but he did not see anyone else. Then, Rael cried out in pain and cupped his forehead with his hands. Rael bent his face to the ground as a scream escaped his lips. Magnus slowed his steps, unsure what he was witnessing. He hid behind a nearby tree-trunk and waited.

Rael finally rose from the ground, and Magnus saw blood drip from his hands. Blood was also smeared on his brother's face. Maybe this would be easier than he thought, *Magnus considered. He took one step from behind the tree, intending to attack his brother before he could recover from his wound.*

Magnus felt a searing pain, and he dropped to his knees, trying to blink the stars from his eyes. Rael turned upon hearing the noise. Magnus looked up at his mother, who now stood over him.

Rael ran over to the pair. "What is going on? Mother, are you alright?" He asked, taking in the blood soaking through the shirt on her left side.

"Rael, you must go. Have you been marked?" She asked quietly. Her breaths seemed painful.

Magnus shook his head as he heard his brother say, "Yes. Just now."

Magnus gazed up at Rosalie as she hugged her Rael and kissed him on the cheek. "Goodbye my son. Live well and beware your brother. I fear he will never stop chasing you."

Rael's eyes widened in understanding. He looked down at Magnus in shock as Rosalie placed her hands on either side of his face. He glowed as if he were a sun. Then, he disappeared.

Magnus roared, and threw himself to his feet. "What have you DONE!"

Rosalie faced her son and responded, "Now you will never find him."

Hatred filled Magnus, and he leaned in closer towards his mother and whispered, "You are finished, old woman."

Magnus blinked twice and exited the dream.

***

When he awoke, he found the chair in front of him empty, and he knew Rael had disappeared the moment Rosalie had touched his face. He stood from his chair and walked to where her body lay as her mind still occupied the dream realm. Magnus picked up the discarded knife and lifted it above her again. He knew what must be done to stop her from interfering in the future.

THIRTY-FOUR

Kenna

After Kenna, Damon, and Ansley had awoken, the elders sprang into action. They eagerly listened as a report was given separately by both Damon and Ansley of the events that had unfolded. Kenna had been moved to the couch, and she didn't wake for several hours after her collapse. In the meantime, Alden and Daro sent messengers to inform the dreamwalkers that the threat had been eliminated. Quinn had suggested that they keep surveillance in each tribe for any cult members that had not been in the building when it collapsed. All agreed this was the best choice. Over the next few hours, the dreamwalkers remained vigilant.

When Kenna finally roused, the elders requested her report of what had happened. She faced the council alone. The worst may have been behind her, but Kenna still found that her hands trembled as she relived the details.

"How were they getting into dreamwalker's dreams?" Daro asked. A wrinkle spread across his forehead, indicating his confusion.

Kenna shook her head. "It still isn't clear, but Dane said he was planning to use me to pull other members of my tribe into the dream. I believe that he was using the tethers between linked dreamwalkers to attack other dreamwalkers."

Daro answered her guess with a frown but kept his thoughts to himself.

"So why did he do it?" Alden inquired. Kenna sighed and brushed her hair back behind an ear, trying to find an explanation she didn't have.

"All I know of Dane is that he was alone. His mother left his family when he was a child, and his father died a few years ago of mysterious circumstances. They think it was undiagnosed heart sickness, but they never examined his body." Kenna saw Quinn raise her eyebrows in Alden's direction. "The only other thing I can say about him is that he was never cruel. He was reliable enough when our tribe needed him, but he was more frustrating than malicious," Kenna finished, wondering what had happened to turn Dane against his own people.

"Cruelty and hatred often hide behind a convincing smile," Daro offered. Quinn and Alden nodded thoughtfully in response. "I'm sorry you had to endure this, Kenna, but I think I speak for all of us when I say that we are in your debt."

Kenna nodded silently, trying to find words to ask the group her most troubling question. "When I was trying to save us...I...I did something impossible. Have you ever seen or heard of anything like it?" She was desperate for answers.

A questioning look grew on Alden's face. "My dear, you are a wielder. You simply built a key, didn't you?"

Kenna shook her head. "The chains were made to prevent our skills from working. I-I-built it from nothing. I *made* it. I *thought* about it, and then our chains broke."

Alden's lips parted as if in shock. His eyebrows lifted behind his spectacles, and then he turned to his brother, Daro. Daro smiled as if he had solved a particularly challenging riddle. "Kenna, are you *elite*?"

"What? Of course not," Kenna replied, trying to hide the quiver in her voice.

"When was your ceremony? From whom did you inherit your skills?" Daro asked.

Kenna sighed in resignation and replied, "Nobody *gave* them to me. I just always had them, I guess. I assumed some of us were born with them. Is that not true?" Kenna asked in a soft voice.

Daro shook his head silently, while Alden and Quinn exchanged surprised glances. "If you did not inherit, then you most certainly *were* born with them, so you are what we call *elite*," Daro concluded. "That makes you the first that I have ever met, and it is my pleasure indeed." Daro bowed his head in Kenna's direction.

Kenna furrowed her brow in deeper confusion. "What does it *mean?* What did I do?" She demanded, raising her voice more than she had planned.

Quinn stood and walked to her. "My dear, it *means* that you have not only one skill but many. The gods blessed you above other dreamwalkers. You do not only build, but it seems you also are unaffected by the parameters of dreams. You can change things others have made without their permissions. That's what happened with the key. You didn't *make* a key, but you imagined one as an answer to the problem you found yourself facing. You unlocked both Damon and yourself, and then you destroyed the building to free all of you."

Kenna stepped back from Quinn, processing. She shook her head as it all began to fall into place.

Quinn added, "It means that you may be the strongest amongst us all." She met Kenna's terrified eyes and raised a hand to pat Kenna's shoulder.

Kenna simply shook her head, taking in the woman's words. *Blessed by the gods?....Strongest of them all?...*

***

After she awoke, Ansley rose from the carpet, eager to find Rhys. She saw him waiting anxiously in the same corner they had been standing in earlier. She took in the bandage on his hand that matched her own and smiled. Ansley ran to him and threw her arms around his neck.

"It worked! Thank you so much for helping me." She lowered her voice, but it wasn't necessary. No one was watching her. The others were crowded around Damon, who was in great need of a healer.

"Did you feel it? You helped me defeat the guards!" She smiled at Rhys, and he nodded in return.

"I did. Good work, Ansley. I am so thankful that you are safe and were successful." His tone seemed changed, but Ansley did not notice. Her heart filled with glee at their combined efforts and success upon joining their skills. She leaned forward and kissed him deeply.

Ansley's joy died when she locked lips with her "savior." A vision hit her hard, pulling her into darkness. The vision held her captive for only a few moments. She was thankful to see that Rhys had noticed no change in her when she pulled away from him.

Instead he merely said, "I must go share the news with our parish. They will be so relieved to hear that Orco's cult has been brought to justice." He kissed her on her forehead before moving away. "I will send a messenger in the morning to see how you are feeling." He flashed a brilliant smile to her that didn't touch his eyes, and Ansley waved goodbye silently. She reached up to touch her lips with a questioning look on her face.

***

That night, Ansley lay on the couch in her grandmother's house, trying to rest after the several difficult days she had faced. Kenna was sleeping in her room, and Damon had been moved to the other spare room. The healers had taken hours to tend to his injuries, both from the scrying and his imprisonment. It seemed that most of his injuries were of a "spiritual" nature, so they took longer to heal.

The healer had mentioned that Damon had lost at least two decades worth of life in his scrying attempt. Damon had only responded to the healer by nodding his head. Ansley was surprised with how quiet he had been since their victory.

She turned onto her side and fluffed her pillow with her hand. Ansley closed her eyes, eager to find the rest she so desperately needed, but then she found herself pulled in a dream she had not meant to venture into…

***

An old woman stood in front of her. The woman was thin but looked strong, and Ansley remembered with a jolt that she had indeed seen this woman before in her trials. The youthful eyes sparkled at her as she recognized this stranger.

"What are you doing here? Who are you?" Ansley demanded as she stepped toward the woman. The woman's grey hair flowed freely in the air that disturbed the darkened room they stood in.

The woman looked at Ansley and finally said, "I am your past and your future, if you aren't cautious."

Ansley did not respond, instead staring at the woman in confusion. The woman continued, "You have made a grave error, young one. You know you have."

Ansley nodded, understanding that the woman before her must be an ancestor of hers. "Are you Rosalie?"

The woman smiled. "So, you did see me in your vision earlier. You should have never entered into that blood oath, young one."

Ansley took a step toward the woman. "How are you here? What are you?"

"I am a wraith trapped in the dream realm because of the actions of the one that you do not recognize. I am neither alive nor dead, but unless I am released, I am destined to remain here forever."

"I have seen Magnus's true face. I saw him for who he really is at last. He has fooled us all with his treachery. How can he dreamwalk like one of us? He has no skill! Is there even a person who is actually named Rhys?" Ansley asked in despair, these questions pouring from her as she tried to understand what was happening around her.

"Yes. You have seen him too, and he needs your help. Magnus will destroy Rhys if you can't save him."

"What do I do?" Ansley cried, falling on her knees in desperation.

"You already know, child. But you must act fast. Magnus knows. The "blood oath" you performed is not what it seems. He will use this bond to destroy all of you."

Ansley raised her face from her hands to glance in horror at Rosalie. "He is your son! Help me!"

"I cannot, child. You must find a way on your own," Rosalie finished. She released Ansley from the dream.

***

Ansley sat up from the couch with a jolt and found tears flowing down her face. Terror gripped her. *What would she do?*

A soft rapping on the wooden door brought her back to reality. Ansley stood from the couch and used the back of her sleeve to wipe the tears from her eyes. She tip-toed to the door, trying not to wake anyone. *Really. Who was knocking at this hour?*

Ansley threw the door open in frustration, both at being disturbed and the dream she had just had. The frustration melted away in an instant, and her mouth fell open in shock. Ansley's eyes grew wide as she stared silently at the man in front of her who stood in tattered traveling clothes and had spatters of mud on his trousers, likely because of the haste he had made in coming here.

"*Rhys?*" Ansley whispered, turning back to look behind her, before shutting the door as she stepped out into the cool night air. The man moved back to allow her some space and shook his head. Those familiar blue eyes and black wavy hair were undeniable, even in the darkest hour of the night.

"No, Ansley. I'm Rhyn, and I've come to help you rescue my brother."

EPILOGUE

The storeroom was cold, and no light entered through the windows. Wooden boards had been nailed over each of them to prevent anyone from spying like the girl had done only a few days earlier. Magnus inspected the empty room before lighting a candle and walking to the stairwell.

The steps creaked noisily with his descent, but even that sound didn't drown out the cries coming from below. He was not worried. Nobody would hear the man. Magnus stepped off the last stair to the dirt floor and passed several tables of metal devices and a set of keys. He approached the wall where the man was hanging from his shackled wrists.

Blood coated the man's exposed, muscular neck from multiple injections made with syringes. The serum had been necessary to ensure he cooperated with Magnus's plan. Used needles lay discarded around him from previous attempts to keep him cooperative. Magnus had given up trying to keep the man quiet once Ansley had been persuaded to leave this place with him.

He now feared that his ruse was at an end with her. But Rhys had been useful in allowing Magnus to gain her trust and make the oath. He would have to remember to reward the necromancer who had helped him find the ancient spell he had used with Ansley for the oath. Thankfully, Ansley was not the least bit suspicious of his idea, and the plan had worked in Magnus's favor.

The man was dressed in tattered clothes, and his wavy black hair had grown shaggy and long enough to cover his ears. His blue eyes had burned with ferocity the first time Magnus had met him, but now the man could barely raise his voice above a whisper. It was likely because of all the shouting he had resorted to in hopes of alerting someone to his presence.

Magnus heard another set of footsteps on the steps. A second man entered the cellar but stood near the top of the stairs to deliver his message. "Magnus, the new recruits are on their way."

"Thank you, Dane. I will be with you shortly."

Dane nodded and turned quickly to ascend the stairs. He favored his left side as he made his way up the stairs. Soon, his steps had faded away. He had been lucky to escape the collapsing building, but he had not exited unscathed. Magnus picked up a knife from a nearby table and walked to Rhys.

"Our plan has worked, and I owe all the credit to you." He said softly. He trailed the end of the knife down Rhys's grimy face and along the edge of his chin, which was now covered in stubble. "She almost didn't fall for it, you know?" He dug the knife in to draw blood and watched it bubble and drip down the Rhys's chin.

Rhys arched his neck before spitting in Magnus's face. "She may have believed you, but you will never succeed," he growled with as much effort as he had remaining. Sparks flew from his eyes.

"But you will *help* me succeed, Rhys. I thought you understood that? You helped me find Ansley. You let me use your face and your skill to lure her in, and now, you will help me convince her to destroy them all. All done in a day's work." Magnus smiled at Rhys as he hung limply from his bonds.

"Why do you need me anymore?" Rhys asked, his voice empty.

"Oh, you know the routine," Magnus replied. "To become a *jinn,* I need a willing subject." He picked up a syringe that had been discarded on the table beside Rhys. "Thanks to your...*cooperation,* I can possess your body and dreamwalk as you do. She may know the truth, but I believe you can persuade her to join our cause." Magnus added, turning back to look at Rhys.

"She does prefer your face to mine, you know," Magnus sneered and tossed the empty syringe on the floor.

"You can't keep me here forever. I will get free, find her, and stop you," Rhys grunted, digging deep for the strength to fuel his voice.

Magnus laughed. "You will never leave here. Not as long as Ansley lives." Magnus turned and dropped the knife on a table once again. He reached his hand to Rhys's exposed neck and dug his nails into the newest looking wound. The man cried out in pain.

"Without you, I can't convince her to listen to me, Rhys. We both know she trusts you enough to do *anything* for you." Magnus rubbed the fresh blood between his fingers before stepping away from Rhys and turning to walk back up the stairs.

"Do what you want with me, but the others will never let you turn her, Magnus." Rhys said, almost in a whisper.

"Just you wait." Magnus replied, laughing to himself as he ascended the stairs and closed the door on the man whose face and skill he borrowed each night to further his dark plan and web of lies.

Brooke Terry

The Gods of the Dreamwalkers

Vito: Creator of the world and "father" of the people

Matrisa: Wife of Vito and "mother" of the people

Cassis: God of war

Amora: God of love

Sophia: God of wisdom

Sali: God of the earth and all things that grow

Caeli: God of the air

Ondo: God of the waters

Kius: God of dreams and sleep who pulls the moon across the sky each night

Poeno: God of justice

Orco: God of death and destruction who delights in struggles of the people and seeks to destroy all that his brother Vito holds dear

Dreamwalker Family Lines of Arvenia

(by constellations)

-The Bear: Blacks

-The Fish: Fischers

-The Serpent: Asps

-The Hunter: Mannes

-The River: Brooks

-The Eagle: Scouts

-The Stallion: Galloways

Lightning Source UK Ltd.
Milton Keynes UK
UKHW012310090223
416755UK00004B/498